JUST LIKE GREY 10

KARL RICHMOND

JESSIE COOKE

WWW.JESSIECOOKE.COM

CONTENTS

A Word from Jessie   v

Chapter 1	1
Chapter 2	7
Chapter 3	14
Chapter 4	19
Chapter 5	26
Chapter 6	31
Chapter 7	39
Chapter 8	46
Chapter 9	53
Chapter 10	58
Chapter 11	64
Chapter 12	69
Chapter 13	74
Chapter 14	79
Chapter 15	85
Chapter 16	91
Chapter 17	98
Epilogue	103

More Books by Jessie Cooke   111

A WORD FROM JESSIE

Just like Grey is an Amazon Best Selling Series.

All books in the series are written for open-minded adults who are not easily offended, so you will encounter anything from cheating, explicit sex, unprotected sex, drug use, adult language, and many more topics that could upset the wrong reader.

These are not vanilla stories.

That said...I hope you enjoy it.

Happy Reading,

Jess

1

KARL

"Oh, you *have* to be fucking kidding me."

"No, sir, this is very real," the lawyer standing before me announced, glaring down at me with a furrow in his brow and a look of clear irritation in his eyes. I got to my feet and started to pace around the spacious office around us, suddenly feeling as though the walls were closing in around me.

"She's really trying to sue me for sexual harassment?" I asked, and the man nodded again.

"That's correct," he replied. "My client, Ms. Isler, is suing you for misconduct while she was working here for your company, and she wishes to resolve the matter in court so both of you can move forward and put this behind you. Unless, of course, you'd like to offer her a payment to make this go away."

I stared at him for a moment. The lawyer – what was his name, Richard something? – looked to be in his forties, a decade or so older than me, and he had that pinched, tight appearance that told me he'd had some work done over the last few years. Guys like that, the people more focused on the way they looked than the job they did, they usually had ulterior motives for getting involved with a case like this one.

"Thanks for taking the time out of your day to deliver the news," I growled to him. "I appreciate it. Really. Now, could you let me get back to work, or is there something else you came by here to tell me?"

"Nothing at all, Mister Richmond," he replied, and I could tell by the tone of his voice that he was enjoying the annoyance right now. Probably thought if he got me pissed, he could use me to wring the big money sponge and get a payoff that would satisfy Kim and get him his percentage, too. Well, he had another thing coming, because I was in no great hurry to do that for him. Or for her, for that matter.

"My secretary will show you to the door," I announced, and I pressed the buzzer to call in Martin, the guy who worked the reception desk outside my door. A moment later, he arrived in the office, and maneuvered Richard whatever-his-name-was out of the room and away from me at last.

I sank back into my office chair and ran a hand through my hair. *Motherfucker.* I couldn't believe she was trying to do this to me. I should have known better, should have known she wasn't just going to let my rejection of her sit without doing anything about it, but I didn't think she would go this far to try to unseat me, and reclaim some of the power she had lost when she had been sitting in this office, clad only in lingerie, waiting for me to arrive so she could seduce me in person.

Kim. Kim fucking Isler. I should have known better than to let her get close to me, than to hire her at all. The Isler family were a long line of assholes, a couple of whom I had worked with before, and if it hadn't been for the fact that her uncle on her mother's side seemed keen to pick up on a deal with me, I would have tossed her application straight in the trash as soon as it had arrived.

But, because I was an idiot and I needed someone to work the mailroom, I had convinced myself it was going to be okay.

Since she was from one of the younger Isler generations, I told myself she would be different from the ones I had met before. Maybe a little kinder, cooler. And when she turned up at the office, she had seemed perfectly passable as a decent employee. She would smile at me in the corridor when we passed one another, and I would usually nod back, too busy to think about much more than just getting out of there so I could make it to the meeting I had next.

Running this place always took up all my attention during the day – I barely spoke to anyone at the office, and I felt like they were all a little scared of me for that reason. But that was why I had managed to build this place from the ground up into the business it was today: Richmond Industries, my family name attached to one of the biggest tech companies in the country. All homemade-American, easy to sell to people who were getting into buying local after so much time going abroad for their cell phones and TVs. It took most of my time and energy just to keep this place ticking over day in and day out, and I wasn't going to throw that away by spending hours chatting with employees I didn't really need to know just out of the goodness of my heart.

Some people might have called me an asshole, and maybe they would have had a point – but it wasn't like I didn't find ways to blow off steam when I was outside of work. There was a reason I had decided to bring this place to life in New York – I had grown up in a little town in Michigan, and I was so ready to get out of there by the time I turned eighteen that I was practically counting down the days when it came around. I hated that place, because I knew there was so much more in the way of what life could offer me outside of it. Not that I didn't appreciate my parents, or my family, or the opportunities they'd given me, but I needed somewhere bigger. Better. Somewhere that was going to let me live the life I knew I needed to, every chance I got.

I had partied my way through college, paid for it all myself by working part-time anywhere that would have me, and by the time I started this place, I already had a reputation as one of the city's most notorious bachelors. Which was fine by me. If it meant that every woman who came up to me in the club already knew I wasn't going to spend my life with her, that just allowed me to cut to the chase and get to the good stuff, right?

It was a reputation, I assumed, that Kim must have heard about when she started working here. I had picked up on a few stories about her when she had first arrived here – nothing too dramatic, just that she had been married a couple of times and she seemed to always be looking for the richest idiot she could find to buckle down with her and give her everything she wanted. But I had dismissed them as gossip, especially since she had gotten a real-ass job by then – reputations stuck for a long time in this city, and I knew that better than anyone.

It had started off quietly with her, just a little flirtation every now and then – she would bring me a coffee in the morning, even when I told her I had a secretary to take care of it.

"I just like being here for you," she replied, fluttering her lashes at me. They looked to be about three inches long, and they were about as fake as everything else about her; I had an eye for plastic surgery, mostly because the same three surgeons performed it on everyone with the cash to afford the good stuff in this city, and I had been with enough women who'd been tweaked and tightened to know the difference. Kim had those puffed-up lips, the fillers in her cheeks that made her face look about two feet wide head-on, and I would have bet that she had the breast implants to match, too, not that I had any intention of finding out. Her body, tiny but enormous in all the right places, was totally out of proportion, looking almost cartoonish in the oddness and fakeness that was clear to see.

I should have shut it down then, but I was too busy to worry too much about someone specific trying to get on my good side. Honestly, I thought she was just vying for a promotion or something, and I ignored it, hoping she would grow bored soon enough of trying to get me to do what she wanted.

But instead, it had gotten more and more intense. She seemed to linger in the corridor outside my office, just waiting for me to walk into her so she could press herself against me. I was sure I was imagining it at first, decided to just ignore it and put it down to my own paranoia, but the more time that passed, the more obvious it became that it was anything other than a mistake. Her dresses were getting lower and lower cut, the skirts riding higher and higher up her hips, until she was practically exposing herself when she bent down to pick up a pen.

I don't know what vibes I must have given her, but she seemed to think her campaign of seduction was actually working against me. That was the only explanation for the fact that she had broken into my office one evening, when I was returning late from a meeting with a new distributor, and draped herself over the desk in nothing but a bunch of expensive, frothy lingerie and a pair of heels.

"Kim, what the hell are you doing!" I demanded, averting my eyes as soon as I stepped through the door.

"I think you know," she purred, and she climbed off the table, a little wobbly in her heels, and took a step towards me. Had she been drinking? I was sure I could smell booze on her, and it was the only thing that would explain a situation as fantastically misjudged as this one.

"Come on, Karl, I know you want this," she continued. I couldn't believe this was happening. I needed to get the hell out of there, and I needed to get *her* the hell out of there, too.

"Put on a damn jacket," I snapped to her. "And get out of my office, Kim. You have no reason to be here."

She stared at me, clearly affronted.

"You're really going to turn down *this?*" she demanded, dramatically gesturing to her own body as though she could hardly believe I had the strength to resist her.

"I really am," I told her. "Now, get out. And don't come back in tomorrow. You're fired."

I kept my eyes pinned to the wall behind her as she reached for the jacket she had divested herself of as soon as she had come through the door – she looked furious, and I ignored her.

As she stalked out of the office and past me, I had been sure this was the last I would hear of her. Because there was no way in hell she was going to dare show her face around here after what she had done, right? But now, three weeks later, she was going to land me in the middle of a lawsuit for sexual harassment – when she knew damn well she had been the one doing the sexual harassing, not me.

I slumped into my chair. Fucking hell. I didn't know what I was going to do next. And I knew there was only one person who could help me make sense of all of this – one person who, I had no doubt, was about to walk through the door at any second, and...

"Karl!" Abi announced, as she pushed the door open without bothering to knock. "What the hell is this I hear about a sexual harassment suit?"

2

ABIGAIL

I stood there in front of him, hands planted on my hips, and he nodded to the door behind me with a defeated expression on his face.

"Could you at least shut the door behind you so not everyone in the office has to hear about this?" he asked me, and I turned and closed it behind me, flicking the lock so nobody else could get in.

"So, tell me, should I be worried that I just locked the door behind me?" I asked him. "Because I just got an email from a lawyer for Kim Isler, who says she's bringing a suit against you for workplace sexual harassment."

"I know she is," he replied, and he let out a long sigh and rubbed his hand over his face.

"And?" I prompted him. "Did something happen between you?"

"Nothing did," he told me, and I could tell he meant it – there was a sureness to his voice that warned me against pressing any further, and I held my hands up and conceded the point.

"I believe you," I replied, and he furrowed his brow at me.

"Do you really?" he asked, and I nodded, and took my usual seat opposite him.

"Karl, I've worked as your head of legal for, what, five years now?" I reminded him. "And this is the first time I've seen a suit that's even anything like this one. If you say nothing happened, and I've got no reason to believe you have a history of this, I believe you. If you weren't doing this five years ago, I don't see why you would start now."

"Good to hear..."

"But I'm not the one you need to convince," I reminded him. "You're going to need to convince a court of that. And I can help you, but I'm going to need you to give me everything I need. You understand?"

As I sat there, opposite the man I worked for, I couldn't help but notice how tired he looked, and I felt a spark of concern down inside of me – concern that was totally misplaced, I knew that, because he was a grown-ass adult and he could take care of himself. But I knew he worked himself stupid-hard, and I didn't want him to burn out. I knew what work in this industry could do to a person. And he didn't deserve that.

In the time I had worked for Karl, I had seen pretty much everyone try to take a piece of him. That was just how it worked when you were at the level of success he was – everyone wanted to prove they were big enough to earn his respect, and, since next to nobody was, that meant most of them just tried to take it from him, instead. It was the sort of attitude that seemed like it ruled this city, this idea that it was just fine to take anything you felt like you were owed, and honestly, it was the one I thrived on, too.

That was why Karl had hired me in the first place, I was sure of it. He could see I had the balls required to make sure this place didn't fall apart under the constant attacks by people trying to take a piece of him. I hadn't had as much experience as some of the other applicants, but he told me I would get it while I was on the job. The two of us had clicked the very first time we had met, and yeah, okay, I would have been lying if I'd said I didn't crush on him for a little bit back then – he was handsome, he was successful, and he believed in me – but I'd gotten over that when I realized he would make a way better employer than he ever would a boyfriend.

Because that's the thing, I saw how he treated the women who worked for him. He was careful around them, respectful, came from that generation who was more aware of what their words could mean to someone who was already nervous. Not to mention the fact I knew what he got up to on the weekends – even now, he would find time to hit the clubs, go out drinking and dancing and hooking up with any woman who looked at him the right way. He was a total playboy, and I had heard plenty of whispers about him from the women in this city – whispers that told me that, while he might have moved on quickly, he knew how to make someone comfortable when they were together. Hardly the actions of someone who was sexually harassing his employees, right?

"Do you have any cameras in here?" I asked him, getting to my feet and pacing back and forth. "She said in the suit that's where it happened. I know they clear them every other week, but..."

"No, no cameras in here," he replied, shaking his head. "Privacy for the meetings, you know. People get antsy if they know you're filming stuff, think you're going to use it against them or something."

"Shit," I muttered. I knew I didn't have to worry about cursing in front of him – the high-pressure nature of this job meant the two of us had seen each other in pretty much every state of disrepair that was possible, and there was no point pretending I was some angel at this stage in the game.

"I think it's easiest just to pay her off and hope it goes away," he remarked. "They offered it to me; that would get it over with."

"And that would mean anyone who wanted a stick to beat you with would have one without looking too far first," I replied. "No, we're not going to do that. You need to focus on keeping yourself out of any situation where people could take it as an admission of guilt – don't worry, that's what I'm here for. I have you covered there. I just need to work out how to do it this time around."

"I don't know," he replied, shaking his head. "Seems like it would be easier to just get this to go away."

"Easier, sure, but that doesn't mean better," I shot back. "I know this is a lot, but you have no history of this on your record, and we're not going to start now. In this climate, even allegations that weren't fully investigated could be all someone needs to dismiss you."

"You're right," he groaned, and he slumped down further in his seat. "Shit, I should never have hired that Isler woman."

"I don't think I even remember her working here," I remarked, furrowing my brow and shaking my head. "Where did she work, again?"

"The mailroom, I think, but she was always hovering around my office, trying to get me to pay attention to her," he replied. "I think she was hoping something would happen between us. She tried to seduce me the night she says I harassed her...that's what this is all about."

"So, she felt spurned and she brought this case against you?" I demanded, and I felt a wash of fury in my guts. I knew I needed to look into this properly before I jumped to any conclusions, but it just made me so mad when I heard about women making shit up like this. I knew maybe I was letting my fondness of Karl cloud my attitude, but I couldn't imagine him doing anything like that – but I could imagine some woman trying to get him into bed to try to ease what she wanted out of him.

"I'm going to do some research tonight," I promised him. "See what I can dig up on her. I'm sure there's something we can use for this case. But don't pay them off, okay? I know how that goes; the last thing you want is someone able to point to that to prove you're an asshole or something."

"You saying I'm not one?" he asked me, grinning playfully. "That's a little sentimental, coming from you."

"Oh, I didn't say you weren't one," I shot back, smiling. "But you're not this kind of asshole, that's for sure. Okay, I need to get back to work – call me if you hear anything else about this, okay? And if any press get in touch, don't speak to them, just pass it on to me."

"You really think they might?" he asked, pulling a face, and I shrugged and nodded.

"If they're trying to stir something up, they might have leaked this to the press already," I warned him. "So stay on your guard. If it gets out, it's because they're trying to push your hand towards paying her, but we're not going to do that. Right?"

"Right," he replied, saluting me like I was his army general. I saluted him right back.

"At ease, private," I joked, and I headed out the door to go back down to the legal department and start going over the particulars of the case that had just arrived on my inbox.

What a way to start a Monday morning. I knew this week was going to be a tough one, ever since I got the call from my mom on Sunday night, the usual harassment I had to deal with from my family every couple of weeks or so about being too focused on my career and not having settled down with a man yet.

"Your sister is going to be engaged soon," she nagged me.

"You could have a nice little house in the suburbs by now, and a couple of children. Doesn't that sound nice?"

"That sounds hellish, Mom," I replied, flicking through the files I had forwarded to everyone for the department meeting the next day.

"You just don't know what you're missing," she told me. I knew she meant well by all of this, but Jesus, it drove me fucking insane when she tried to pressure me. Having a husband and kids was what she had always wanted for herself, ever since she had been a little girl, but I had always wanted to work – the legal profession was one of the toughest out there, so I had known I was going to need to commit to it totally if I wanted to get anywhere, especially as a woman. But that didn't seem to satisfy my mother, and she would regularly call me up to see if I had given in and at least checked out the men available at the sperm bank.

"I guess I don't," I replied. There was no point in arguing with her. I just had to let her go off for a little while and tell me my life wouldn't be fully worth living until there was a baby in my arms and a husband by my side. I knew it drove her crazy that I had moved all the way out here, to the big city, and I hadn't even met *one* man that I had brought home to the family. I was just way too busy for that – way too busy to date, and way too busy to deal with the egos of guys who couldn't handle the fact I made more money than them. Of which there were way too many for my liking.

"You shouldn't spend so much time at the office, you're missing out on so much," she continued to talk to me, and I tuned her to the back of my head for the time being. This was precisely the shit I didn't need to hear right now. I was busy with trying to get the details together for a new launch Karl was going to be selling at the end of the month, and I didn't want to have to deal with the baby-pressure-valve that was my mother going off in my ear every time I tried to think straight.

"How are you guys, anyway?" I asked her, once she had seemed to calm down. Even though they only lived across the state, it was hard for me to get down there and see them that often because of work, and I knew it drove my mom crazy that I didn't get down more often. I missed them, I did, but sometimes the slow movement in the small town was enough to make me feel like I was losing my damn mind. I just couldn't move at that pace, not any longer, not since I'd had a taste of what it was to go as if the river was sweeping you right along off your feet.

"We're fine," she replied. "Thinking of you. And the fancy job of yours. We're proud of you, you know that, Abigail?"

"I know," I replied, and I smiled. I knew they were glad I had been able to do what I wanted. It was just a lot for them to get their head around the fact it was *all* that I wanted. I wasn't one of those women who felt the urge to prove I could have it all and then some. If I only ever had this job, my friends, my family, then I would be happy. I didn't need to bother with adding another branch to the family tree in my own right, that was for sure.

But as soon as the call had come in, I'd known I was doomed for a rough week. And the one that lay ahead? Yeah, it was rougher than anything I could have imagined. But I was a good lawyer, I knew that much, and I wasn't going to let anything throw me off my game. I was going to send this case down the river, and we were going to be able to forget about it once and for all, and that was the only thing I was going to focus on until this damn thing was behind us for good.

3

KARL

I waved down the waiter to get another glass of wine, as Alana, my best friend, sat opposite me. Her mouth was hanging open, and she looked as though she had been hit by a truck.

"So she's really suing you?" she asked me, and I nodded, shaking my head, still not quite sure any of this was real.

"Yeah, she really is," I replied with a sigh. "I can't believe it. I thought I had seen the last of her when I kicked her out of the office, but seems like she's going to keep making a nuisance of herself as long as she can."

"Jesus Christ," Alana muttered, running her hand over her short buzz-cut of hair – she had shaved it all off last year, because she was sick of getting mistaken for a straight girl, and these days, I didn't think anyone could make that mistake.

"And all because you rejected her?" she asked. I nodded.

"That's the only reason I can think of," I replied. "It sounds crazy, but I don't see what else she could have against me. It seems like she's just been holding off until she could get her lawyer in place, and now she's got him, it's going to be lights-out for me."

"What a bitch," Alana said, as she picked at one of the sushi rolls in front of her.

"You know you're meant to eat that in one bite, right?" I teased her, and she rolled her eyes at me.

"Aren't you meant to be all small-town bumpkin?" she asked me. "I'm the one who grew up here, remember?"

"Yeah, and you could start acting like it," I teased her right back. She shook her head at me. I knew I drove her crazy, and I knew she wouldn't have had it any other way. The two of us had met when we had been in college together, both studying business – she was a co-owner of a little shop on the West side, a clothing store that she ran with a gay guy that catered mostly to other people in that community, and the two of us had remained fast friends into adulthood. I liked having women around, and doubly so when I knew they were women I couldn't fuck up by getting drunk and falling into bed with them.

"So what are you going to do about it?" she asked me with interest, once the waiter had come to top up my wine – we were out at this little sushi place, somewhere not far from my apartment. I had thought about going out and getting drunk and trying to forget all of this, but I figured it was for the best to keep myself focused on what the hell was happening, not stirring up more questions about my reputation and what I was getting up to in this town.

"I thought it would make the most sense to just pay them off," I replied. "But Abi..."

"Oh, Abigail?" Alana replied, perking up at once. "The girl who runs your legal department?"

"Yeah, that's the one."

"She's so cute," Alana sighed happily. "And so straight. You know, you're so lucky, being a guy, not having to wonder if every hot girl is even into your gender."

"I'm sure plenty of guys feel just as annoyed when they see you," I remarked, and she laughed.

"Okay, good save," she replied, and she took a sip of her sake. I couldn't help but reflect on what she had said for a moment. I had worked with Abi for so long now that I supposed I didn't even think about the way she looked, but it was true – Abigail was gorgeous. I had noticed it the very first time we had met, and maybe that had more than a little influence on the fact that I wanted to keep her around. With her long red hair, those sharp green-gray eyes, and a smattering of freckles on her nose that showed up when she wasn't concealing them, she was seriously cute. I tried not to let my mind linger on that for too long. Last thing I needed was to start feeling attracted to someone I worked with, given the mess I had already landed myself in just giving another one the time of day.

"So you're going to fight this in court?" Alana asked, and I nodded.

"Yeah, that's the plan," I replied. "I don't know how it's going to go down, but Abi reckons we should put up a fight. That paying them off would just wind up in more trouble for the company in general."

"I think she's right," she agreed.

"You'd say that about anything she said," I teased her. "Because you think she's cute."

"And what's wrong with that?" she demanded with a laugh. "Just because I'd do anything that a pretty woman says doesn't mean my opinions are worth any less..."

We spent the rest of the night in our usual banter, and, soon enough, it was time for me to head home and get some sleep – I was a little tipsy by the time I headed back through the door to my apartment, and I figured a shower was in order to wash some of this day right off my back.

As I turned on the hot water, I yawned and started to strip

down, and found my mind drifting back to Abigail once more. The two of us had worked together for long enough now that we had built up a really solid rapport, and I felt like I could have trusted her with anything that came my way. Okay, so maybe it was going to be tough, navigating our way through this mess together, but as long as I had her there, to believe in me and make sure I didn't fuck this up, I knew it was going to be fine.

As I stepped under the warm water and let it cascade over me, I closed my eyes, and found my head filled with an image – a woman on my desk, in nothing but lingerie once more. But instead of Kim, this time it was Abi.

I could see her so vividly it was almost like the image was right there in front of me. And I reached out to touch her, to skim my fingers over that perfect, pale body of hers, and watched as she reacted – her red hair loose, tumbling around her shoulders, her lips slightly parted as though she could hardly wait for more. I would trace my fingers up her belly, over her breasts, and dip them into her mouth, and she would seal her lips around them at once and start to suck obediently, eyes wide and tongue swirling around them at once. The other hand between her legs, I would push her thighs apart, and then guide my fingers down, down, down, pushing them roughly into her panties, against her pussy, so I could feel just how wet she was for me...

And it was in that moment I snapped back to reality. Alone in the shower. Just me. No Abi. Nobody at all, in fact. And my cock was hard, demanding attention; the thought of her like that, a gift laid out all for me, was more than I could handle.

I finished cleaning myself off, waiting for the erection to fade, and cursed myself for letting Alana get into my head. Abi was just someone who worked for me, that was it. The person who worked for me who was going to make sure I didn't get into more trouble for this case than I needed to, actually. And that was the most important thing for the time being – that I remembered just who she was and what she was going to do for me. Not that I spent any more time picturing her in panties and a bra splayed out on my desk for me...

Shit. I was going to need to blot that image from my mind. Maybe another glass of scotch would do it? Well, I had no idea if it was going to work, but it was worth a try. I poured myself a glass and took a long sip, and stood there at the window, looking down over the city below. And wondering if, somewhere, Abi was doing just the same thing as me.

4

ABIGAIL

I yawned and took a long sip of the coffee that my assistant Greta had brought to my desk that morning before I had arrived. I had been up all night putting together the plan of attack for this lawsuit, and now I felt like I needed nothing more than to crawl back into bed and pretend I wasn't going to be in the office at all today.

But I needed to stay focused – if we were going to beat this thing, then I had to make sure he understood just how serious it was, and that this was going to be a matter of reputation as much as anything else. And we had to make sure his reputation stayed as peaceful and un-notable as we could during this time. I had no idea how it was going to work, but I was sure as hell going to try. Because being his lawyer right now meant being his full-blown PR team, too, and I was going to make sure he understood just what he needed to do so all of this fell into place.

I knew he wasn't going to be happy about the thought of the restrictions we were putting into place on his social life, but it was for the best. I had no idea how much I would need to delve in to get things clear, but I wanted to be certain nobody had a reason to even glance sideways at the way he chose to live his life. People were going to be looking for anything in the way of corroborating evidence that he was a total sleaze, and the last thing I wanted was for a single one of them to get their hands on it.

Because I knew the way we people looked at him – I could still remember when I had started working for him, and my best friend and then-roommate Bella had basically pinned me to the wall to ask about what he was like.

"Because he's a total playboy, isn't he?" she had asked me. "Was he flirting with you? Was he hot? Did he act like he was single?"

"I have no idea," I protested, laughing as I ducked past her to get myself something to drink.

"Yeah, but you never do," she replied, rolling her eyes at me and shaking her head. "You can never tell if a guy's flirting with you unless he sends it to your work email so you can't miss it."

"Point taken," I agreed, and I felt a little flutter in my chest. Because yes, okay, Karl was pretty cute – with that short dark hair, the stubble on his jaw, his blue eyes that lit up when he smiled. He was wiry, strong, the kind that came from actually going out and doing shit instead of just standing around the gym lifting weights and hoping for the best.

"But he's my boss," I pointed out to her. "Nothing's going to happen between us, anyway. That's all that matters."

"Oh, you're no fun," she replied, pulling a face. I knew she was right, but there was no way I was going to fuck up a good job now that I finally had one by letting myself get caught up in some crush on the man I was working for.

And, these days, I was so far removed from that crush I could hardly remember it in the first place. That was what happened when you saw the guy you might have once thought was cute was going through women at a crazy-ass rate, leaving this trail of them in his path, most of whom spent all their time longing for him, wishing they could have been the one who he had changed for. And I hated to break it to those chicks, but there was no way in hell he was going to change at this point in the game. He had been doing this for far too long now, and nothing was going to stop him from living life the way he wanted to.

Except, maybe, this lawsuit. Only temporary, for sure, but hopefully, I could convince him to take a little time off. I didn't know how much he was going to have to drop, but I got the feeling he was hardly going to be happy about it. Right now, that wasn't my problem. I just wanted to get this under control, and I needed him to work with me to make it happen.

So, as soon as I heard he was in his office, I headed down there, strode in, and locked the door behind me to make sure we weren't going to be disturbed.

"Hey, Abi," he greeted me, and his eyes slid away from making contact with mine – huh? What was that about?

"What's up?" I asked, and he shook his head.

"Nothing," he replied swiftly. "Just hung over, that's all."

"Yeah, about that," I replied, planting myself down in the seat opposite him. "I've been putting together our game plan for how we're going to approach this case, okay? And first things first, I think you need to take a break from the bar scene for a while. A long while, preferably."

He looked up at me, his eyes wide, and it was almost comical how spooked he looked by the very *suggestion* of what I was saying.

"You're serious?" he demanded, and I nodded.

"Deadly serious," I replied. "I think we need to focus on reputation management, and this seems like the best way to start. We make sure you're not being caught in any compromising positions with any women, and there's nothing the other side of this case can pull on to make you look bad."

"How long is this going to last?" he asked, defensively.

"At least a few weeks, maybe longer," I replied. "As long as it takes us to get this case kicked out of court and dealt with once and for all. Do you think you can handle that?"

"It doesn't sound like you're giving me much of a choice," he said, shaking his head. "What am I going to do to fill the evenings? I always go out..."

"You're going to stick it out in the office with me to work on the case," I told him firmly. "Shouldn't be too difficult."

"You make it sound like I've just been waiting for the excuse to spend time with you," he teased. "You sure you're not angling to bring a case against me yourself?"

"And get myself fired in the process?" I protested. "Hell, no. Now, come on, tell me everything you can about what happened the day you said she tried to seduce you. The more we have on her, the more likely we are to be able to make this go away once and for all..."

And, just like that, he launched into everything that had happened the night Kim had tried to get him into bed with her. Honestly, if he was telling the truth, and I had no reason to think he wasn't, then she had some serious balls on her. I don't think I would ever have had the nerve to do something as brazen as that. I guess, when it came to sex, I was more likely to let the people who wanted it from me come looking for it, as opposed to putting it out there for them to take.

Which would maybe explain why I had failed to get laid for the last year. Maybe longer. I tried not to think about it too much, because I just got so down on myself when I allowed my brain to stray to that part of my life, but I was starting to get a little needy for it. I wasn't sure who I was craving it from, exactly, but the more that work stress seemed to pile up, the more I found myself needing the release that came from just allowing someone to take me. Sometimes a girl just needed a really good fucking, you know, and the more time that passed without one, the surer and surer I became it was all I was really missing from my life. My family might have thought it was a man or a husband or something, but really, it was just someone who was able to take control and make me come in the process...

"So, do you think that's enough to work with for now?" Karl asked me, and I blinked and realized I was still very much in his office right now. Still very much at work. I managed to nod, hoping that somewhere in the back of my head, I had been able to take in everything he had just said to me.

"I think so," I replied, and I got to my feet quickly. "Sorry, I just need to grab something from my desk, alright? I'll be back in a minute..."

"Of course," he replied. "I'm not going anywhere."

I smiled, and then headed out of his office and towards the bathrooms at the end of the corridor. As soon as I was inside, I locked a cubicle behind me, and slumped against the wall.

"Jesus," I said to myself. What was happening to me? I had allowed my need to get the better of me, and that was the last thing I wanted right now. It was important I kept my head in the game. Not just for my job, but for everyone else's here – if Karl really was landed in hot water for all of this, then the whole company could go down with him. There was no way in hell I was going to let some horny little part of my brain get the better of me and send the rest of it crashing down around me.

And so, the decent thing to do would be to make myself come and get this over with so I could focus on what needed to be focused on. Leaning up against the wall, I unbuttoned my pants and pushed my hand into my panties, closing my eyes as I focused on the slick little nub of my clit beneath my clothes.

I pressed my lips together to keep from making a sound. I wasn't sure I wanted to be busted in the middle of this, not when there were questions of sexual harassment floating around the office. And how would it look, anyway? If I had gone straight from my boss's office to the bathroom to get myself off. People would think he was the reason I was standing here with my hand down my panties right now, even though I knew it was nothing to do with that...

Suddenly, it was almost as though I could feel him against me. I could sense the aftershave he used, that classic, ocean-scented masculine one that always made me want to ask where he had gotten it. He always had the perfect amount of dark stubble on his sharp jaw, and I knew it would have grazed my skin if he had kissed me – I felt a flood of want between my legs and knew this was getting me where I needed to go. Planting one foot on the closed lid of the toilet, I let my mind wander as far and as fast as it wanted, knowing I had shit to take care of and certain it would be easier just to let myself fantasize wildly.

In my head, he pushed me against the wall, pulling down my pants so he could expose me. He was strong, I knew that much, and the thought of that strength aimed squarely at me was enough to make my entire body feel like it was flicking on to fire mode. He wouldn't wait, wouldn't hold back, turning me around so he could get to me. His hands on my hips, he yanked me back towards him, so he could see my glistening pussy, ready for his cock. Maybe he would push his fingers inside of me, teasing me about how wet I already was for him, while I silently pleaded with him to give me what I wanted, what I knew I needed...

And then he pushed into me. Hard. Rough. The sort of fucking that told me this wasn't about me, this was about him, about him taking what he wanted and making sure I kept up in the process. He pulled my hips back on to him so he could get inside me deep, and the image of it was so vivid in my head I could nearly feel it. My skin ached and my body burned, and I rubbed my clit harder, pushing a finger inside of me so I could mimic the feeling of his dick filling me up. Oh, God, it was so real I could almost sense it – thick, wide, spreading me open. His voice in my ear, telling me to *take it, take it, take it...*

When I came, I had to press my lips together to keep from crying out in orgasm. I didn't want anyone to know I was in here, even less wanted them to figure out what I was doing here, and I let out a gasp instead, stilling my fingers in my panties and trying to slow myself down before I slipped to the floor below me. That had been...intense. How long had it been since I had given myself an orgasm like that? I pulled up my pants, buttoned them again, and flushed the toilet just in case anyone might have been listening.

As nonchalantly as I could, I went outside to wash my hands, and checked myself out in the mirror. My cheeks were a little flushed, and my lips were moist where I had been panting as I had gotten closer to the edge. I splashed a little cold water on my face, hoping it would be enough to get me to calm down a little, but I wasn't sure if it was working. The last thing I needed was for him to work out, when I walked into his office once more, that I had just been masturbating right there in the office – because I imagined he had seen enough women who had just come to know what it looked like when he saw it.

I couldn't believe he had been the one to cross my mind when I had been doing that. What was that about? Was it just because he was the guy I happened to spend the most time around? Yeah, it had to be something like that, didn't it? Nothing more to it than that. Because there was no way that, after all this time, I was starting to feel an attraction to him all over again. We worked together, and we were working together right now on a case that was more sensitive than most. The last thing I needed was for my emotions to get the better of me. And I was going to make damn sure that they did nothing of the sort.

5

KARL

I PACED BACK AND FORTH IN MY APARTMENT, TRYING TO BURN OFF the excess energy that felt like it was going to set me on fire from the inside out.

Was this what it was going to be like as long as I was under house arrest? Because if it was, I fucking hated it. I fucking hated the way it made me feel, being stuck behind these four walls. I had already gone to the rock-climbing wall in an attempt to blow off some steam, but that had just gotten me hot and bothered and now I needed something else to get my head clear of the mess that was going on in there right now. What the fuck was wrong with me? I had no idea, but what I did know was that this was going to be one hell of a difficult month.

I knew Abi was right, though. The more time I could spend flying under the radar, the better. People were going to be watching me like a hawk from here on out, and I wanted nothing more than to just blow off some steam the way I always did, by heading out to the club and having a good time and trying to forget the rest of the world existed for a little while. It might not have been how everyone did it, but it was how it had always worked for me, and I didn't see why I should have to give that up just because someone had brought some false accusations against me. I was being punished for something I didn't do, like when my brother had smashed the back window of our house and had blamed me and gotten me grounded for a month.

I could have used this time to reach out to my family, of course, but in truth, I wasn't really feeling like talking to them right now. I knew they would have heard about the case by now – they spent as much time as they could trying to track down every little detail of my life to prove things weren't as perfect as I made them out to be down in New York. Of course, they didn't seem to realize that, every time they did that, I was ten times more likely to clam up and act like everything was just the way I wanted it to be.

But hell, the last thing I needed right now was one of them lording it over me about how I had managed to get myself in trouble once again. Martin, my brother, he would have been quick to come up with some point about how if I had gotten married, like him, these sorts of cases would never have come up, because people would never believe a married man would do something so heinous. Much as I tried to point out to him that a lot of married men actually *did* do shit like that, he seemed to think the ring on his finger was a cure-all for anything people might have held against him.

They all thought I should have settled down by now. Of course, the fact I had gotten a business up and running and off the ground didn't count as settling down to them. No, they wanted something more than that – proof I was planning on knocking someone up, a woman I could bring to family dinners, shit like that. Shit that bored the hell out of me, because I struggled to keep interest in someone for more than a couple of nights at most.

It wasn't that I didn't like them as people. Most of the time, I did – I had a hard time getting it up for someone who I thought was a total bitch, and most of the women I slept with were fun, cool, clever, as well as being hot as hell. But I knew there was something they couldn't give to me, something I wasn't willing to go the rest of my life without, and that was a deal-breaker when it came down to it.

Ever since I had first arrived here, I had known I needed it. That passion. That need – the willingness to submit. I supposed it was something that was a hangover from my work, really, that need to be with someone properly, to have someone who would allow me to take complete control of them when we were in bed together. If the girls I hooked up with were down for it, I would try a little of this and that – some of them even talked a big game about everything that they could do, got me excited, sure that I had finally met the person that wanted to do this the way I did.

But then I would get them into bed, and all they would want was to get a little spank here and there and loll about not doing much while I tried to get them into it. That's what they thought submission was, really – just not doing anything at all. As much as I tried to encourage them. It seemed like they had learned it from pop culture, from the bullshit films and books that tried to make it look like it was such a boring thing. They played innocent and they wanted me to do all the work for them, when that was far removed from what I needed.

The more thought I had given it, the more it had become clear to me that their submission didn't mean much to me because they didn't have much power to give up in the first place. The majority of them were younger than me, spent a lot of time clubbing, socialites living off their parents' money and not much more than that. Nothing wrong with it, of course. But I needed something more. I needed some*one* more than that. I didn't know exactly what it was I was looking for, but I was certain it came wrapped in a more distinctive package than most of the girls I spent bringing home to this place night after night.

It was like an itch I couldn't scratch – hooking up with all those girls, it felt like I got close, but I was still searching for the one who clicked with me. The one who was powerful, strong, who had everything going for her, but still wasn't afraid to give that power to me for a while when we were together. It was hard to find, it seemed, given that I had been looking for years and hadn't found anyone who gave me what I needed. And it was only going to get harder now that I was basically under house arrest and unable to get out into the real world to find what I was looking for.

But those were the orders I was under, and that was just what I was going to have to live with for the time being. It might have already been driving me crazy, but I didn't have much of a choice. There was no way in hell I was going to let any of this tank my business, not after I had worked so hard to get it off the ground in the first place. Kim Isler might have been sure she could get what she wanted from me, but she had another thing coming – I was going to make sure she never dared make the same mistake again.

And it was good to know Abi believed in me as much as she did. She had taken my word for it right from the start, and it seemed like if she bought my story, then we would be able to sell it to other people, too. To the people who needed to hear it. I had no idea how this was going to go, not really, but I knew I was going to find a way to survive it and keep my business afloat no matter what happened. It was purely a matter of time until this was all wrapped up and dealt with, and then I could get back to reality once more.

But in the meantime...in the meantime, I had to find some way to keep my need from getting the better of me. I couldn't find anyone to bring back here, and I had no intention of going over old ground and hitting up women I had already been with. I didn't know how I was going to keep my head, but I would have to find a way to make it work, because I had no choice but to keep my shit in hand and keep myself from doing something I shouldn't have. It was for the good of my future. And I wasn't going to put that at risk, not after I had worked so hard to secure it.

The only woman in my life who mattered right now, I told myself, was Abigail. And that was just the way it was going to have to stay. No matter how much I might have wanted something more than what I was getting.

6

ABIGAIL

I TOSSED AND TURNED IN BED THAT NIGHT, UNABLE TO THINK about anything but the case. And I wondered if this was what it felt like to lose your mind, because I was pretty sure I was going to have a hard time getting back to reality after everything I was dealing with.

I had started to look into Kim, but I hadn't been able to find anything about her. As in, nothing at all. Not just that she hadn't done much before she had started working for Karl, but she didn't seem to have done a damn thing at all, and I had to admit, there was something bugging me about that. Something was wrong there, wasn't it? I was sure there was something off about all of this, off about the way she conducted herself, and I just needed to figure out what it was.

I had been up all night trying to piece together what was setting off alarm bells inside my head, but I hadn't been able to come up with a damn thing. I was starting to worry now, starting to worry that I might not find what I needed to show her up the way I had to. Because there had to be something she was hiding, and I needed to find out what it was before she took down Karl for good. And sent the rest of the company crashing down around him.

In all honesty, I was starting to wonder just how much of this was about my job for me. Yes, I didn't want to end up out on the streets and unemployed, but truthfully, I knew it wouldn't take me long to find someone else who would be happy to take me in and give me a job after I had proved my mettle under Karl for so long. No, this was about Karl. I was sure of it – and I knew the last thing I needed to cloud my vision right now was loyalty to the man I was meant to be protecting. I had to look at this situation neutrally, and, if I failed to pull that off, then all of this could come crashing down around my ears before I could stop it. And I would only have myself to blame.

I peeled myself out of bed and paced my apartment, glad that I didn't have any roommates to worry about. Anyone I lived with right now would have been going crazy with how much I was up during the night, trying to figure out whatever it was that Kim was managing to keep under wraps. But there wasn't anyone I could talk to about this, anyway – nobody I could even come close to discussing the details of this case with, lest they take it to the press and use it to expose Karl's secrets and force his hand one way or another.

There was only one person I could talk to about all of this. And that person just so happened to be Karl Richmond.

Fuck it. I needed to speak to him. I knew it was probably a bad idea, given that it was two in the morning, but I had to tell him the dead end I had come up against when I had been looking into Kim. Maybe he could shed some light on it. And, if he had any sense, then he wouldn't be sleeping any more than I was right now.

I dialed his number, and it rang a couple of times before he picked up; he sounded wide-awake when he answered the phone, much to my surprise.

"Hey, Abi," he greeted me.

"Karl, we need to talk," I told him quickly.

"Sounds serious."

"It is. Or, it might be. Where are you right now?"

"At home, but I could be at your place in ten minutes if you need me there."

"I think I do," I admitted. "You have my address, right?"

"I sure do," he replied. "See you in a minute."

"See you," I echoed after him, and I hung up the phone before I could think better of what I had just done. I had no idea if this was a good idea or not, but frankly, I knew I needed to see him. I just hadn't quite figured out yet if it was about the case or not.

What else would it be about? The lawyer in me started arguing before I could stop her, but I knew she was just putting up a fight against nothing. I could feel it, at the back of my mind, something that went further than just loyalty to my boss. I had known Karl for years now, and it had been a long time since I had first felt the flush of attraction to him, the one I had dismissed because I knew there was nothing good to come from something like that. But I missed him. I missed that version of him like crazy. The one my friends had teased me about, the one who grinned at me across the desk and made my heart spin.

And working with him so closely again, I felt sure this was the version of him I was dealing with once more. I had found him. Uncovered him again. And now we were spending all our time together, working towards a common goal, I knew there was nothing I could do to stop myself.

I poured myself a drink – vodka on the rocks, hardly professional, but I hardly cared. All that mattered to me was that I was around him and I didn't stop pushing forward with this case for an instant. I needed this. I needed him. I needed to look him in the eyes and tell him that no matter how many people thought badly of him, I would always believe in him. I trusted him.

The need that had been rising up inside of me, the need I thought I had sated with my hands down my panties when I had been in the bathroom of the office, it was back. And when I heard the buzz on my door, I knew it was all trained on him, as much as I wanted to pretend I was beyond that, better than that, smarter than that. I hated this. I hated that I couldn't stop myself wanting him. I hated that I was here, in the middle of the night, allowing my mind to stray to the one place it should never have gone.

I went to the door, buzzed him up, threw back the last of my drink. There was only one way this was going to happen, and that was if my inhibitions were low and I finally gave myself over to the want that had been moving inside of me all this time.

When he appeared in front of me, I almost chickened out. I didn't know what I had done, bringing him here, but he was right in front of me and I knew there was nothing else that would do to put out the fire that had been burning bright inside of me all this time.

Luckily, I didn't need to say the words out loud to him. He seemed to figure it out as soon as he laid eyes on me; he moved towards me, grabbing me by the hips, pulling me towards him roughly, so my body was pressed against his. He looked deep into my eyes, as though searching to make sure this was what I wanted.

"Tell me you want this," he said to me, and I nodded.

"I want this," I breathed back. And, with that, he leaned down and planted a kiss on my lips, and I finally felt the hunger that had been burning inside of me begin to sate itself. This was what I had needed all along, even if I had been too nervous to admit it to myself. Him. Him. Him.

He pushed me over the threshold and closed the door

behind us, and I guided him towards my bedroom as quickly as I could, not wanting to waste a moment of the time we had here together. I knew I should have stopped this before it went any further, but I saw it as being just like the moment I'd had back at the bathroom at work – a chance for me to get out of my head and just have a good time for a change, instead of getting so caught up in what I thought I needed to do.

I pulled him down on top of me, the weight of him pushing down into the messy covers of my bed; to think, I had been lying there tossing and turning and with no idea what the hell I was meant to do next, and I could have just called him and told him to come over and he would have done it in an instant. I kissed him hard, passionate, my tongue in his mouth, the roughness of his stubble against my cheek, feeling his cock beginning to stir against my hip. He had been thinking just the same thing as me, lying in bed and imagining what it would have been like to take me this way. And that was enough to get me dangerously needy for his cock.

"Fuck me," I whined in his ear, not sure where that voice had come from but not interested in stopping it.

"I'll tell you when you get to fuck me," he whispered back, and the dominance in his voice was enough to send a shiver down my spine. Okay, so this was a guy who knew just what he wanted and wasn't afraid to make it pretty damn clear, and there was no way I was going to go arguing with him. I felt the last vestiges of protest wither inside of me, giving in to how sure he was.

"Turn over," he growled in my ear, and, when I didn't move fast enough for his liking, he grabbed me by the hips and flipped me over in the bed – he was so much stronger than I had imagined he would be, and knowing he could have done anything to me that he wanted sent another surge of want through my system.

He ripped down the pajama pants that I was wearing, leaning down to sink his teeth into my ass and making me squeal – he was rougher than I had imagined he would be, but I was surprised to find I liked it. I spent all day at work being the one in control; maybe there was something to be said for sacrificing a little of that every now and then...

He pushed two fingers roughly into my pussy, and I gasped and grasped for the covers to ground me back in the real world.

"God, you're so wet," he said, and he brought his fingers to my mouth and traced my syrupy wetness across my lips, dipping them into my mouth so I could taste them. I closed my eyes and sucked on his fingers obediently, unable to think about anything but how much I wanted him inside of me, just how long he was going to make me wait before he finally gave that to me once and for all.

"Condom," he ordered me, and I reached into my bedside cabinet and pulled one out, handing it to him as I lifted my hips from the bed. This angle had always been my favorite, and, doing it this way, maybe I could kid myself that I wasn't in the middle of fucking the man I was meant to be working for.

I heard the rip of the condom and felt myself tense with anticipation, and, a moment later, the pressure of his cock pressing against the entrance to my pussy. I gasped with relief. Oh, my *God.* That felt so good, I could hardly think straight. He took his time easing himself inside of me, going slow, taking his time, and I gripped on to the covers for dear life, reminding myself that yes, this was really happening, and yes, this was really Karl inside of me right now.

"God, you feel good," he murmured, as his hands came to my hips to pull me back against him, enveloping the last inch or so of his cock inside of me. One hand slipped down the length of my spine, winding into my hair, and he tugged lightly so I was turned around to look at him.

And, with his eyes on mine, he began to fuck me.

Long, slow strokes at first, as though he was letting me get used to the feeling of him thrusting inside of me, but once he seemed sure I was ready for it, he started to go harder. I could feel his body tensing against mine, and I could see the need written all over his face as he continued to take me in long, hard strokes, filling me all the way to the very brim with his beautiful cock. My jaw hung open, and my eyes started to blur around the edges as I tried to make sense of what was happening to me right now. Nothing mattered. Nothing mattered but how good he felt inside of me, and how much more of this sweetness I could take before I tipped over the edge and into the relief that I needed so fucking badly.

He moved his hand between my legs and started to play with my clit as he took me, going hard and fast, the only sound in the room that of our breath and our skin coming together, over and over again. I could feel myself cresting towards the edge, arching towards the release I knew I needed so badly, and sure enough, it didn't take long until I was there, edging on what I needed, on what I wanted...

"You close?" he asked me, voice hoarse.

I nodded.

"Say it," he ordered me.

"I'm...I'm close," I managed to get the words out.

"Then come," he said, and, at the sound of his words, I finally felt myself giving in and tipping helplessly over the edge and into my release.

The sensation was incredible, more than I could take for a moment, the pleasure demanding every inch of my attention – I felt his cock twitch inside of me as he finished a few seconds later, but I was so focused on my own release I could hardly take notice of it. I groaned loudly, unable to contain myself, letting out a cry that must have woken every one of the neighbors as he continued to move inside me – slower than before, but not showing me any mercy, stretching out the orgasm as long as I could take it.

And frankly, I didn't want this to be over. Because, as soon as it was, I was going to have to deal with the fact I had hooked up with the man I worked for, and that everything in my life had just gotten one whole hell of a lot more complicated.

7

KARL

I sat there, in my office, looking at the clock. I had a meeting with Abigail at ten that morning, and I had no idea whether or not she was going to actually turn up.

I wouldn't have blamed her if she hadn't. After all, the last time I had seen her was when the two of us had been fucking like animals in her apartment, and I got the feeling she was hardly going to be a fan of picking up where we had left off.

Which was a hell of a shame, because I could tell we had some pretty damn crazy chemistry between us. What we had shared – look, okay, I had hooked up with a whole lot of women in this city, and even I could see we had something pretty special going on between us. Something that wasn't going to be easily shaken. Being with her had been intense, more intense than anything I'd had in a long time, maybe just because I hadn't *had* anything else in a long time. But I knew just as well that it made things one hell of a lot more complicated, and she was probably going to walk through that door and tell me we needed to put a stop to shit right then and there before anything got more complicated than it needed to be.

And she had a point. I was meant to be fighting a case right now about sleeping with someone I worked with. Going ahead and doing just that was hardly going to make me look innocent now, was it? No matter how good it had been. No matter how hot our chemistry. No matter how much I wanted to just go right back over to her place, throw her down on to the bed, and slam into her again, just to watch her squirm...

The door opened, and I blinked and pulled myself out of the fantasy of my memory for a moment. And there she was – the very woman I couldn't get out of my mind. In the flesh.

"Hey," she greeted me, as she slipped over the threshold. I could have been imagining it, but did I see a little flush to her cheeks right now? I had never seen her blush in all the time I had known her, and I had to admit, it was pretty damn cute.

"Hi," I replied, and she closed the door behind her and took her usual seat opposite me. Normally, she was the picture of confidence, but today, she looked as though she wished the ground would open up and swallow her.

"So," she began, and that pink flush to her cheeks seemed to increase a little.

"So," I replied. And she let out a giggle and shook her head.

"Shit, I'm sorry," she said. "I don't...it's been so long since I've been with someone that I don't know what to say right now."

"So, we're actually acknowledging what happened now?" I asked, and she nodded.

"Yeah, I guess that we are," she replied. "It's...it was good. I want you to know I don't regret it. I had a really good time, I hope you did, too."

"I did," I agreed, and she smiled at me. God, she had the cutest fucking smile I had ever seen in my life. It was hard for me to resist leaning over the table and planting a kiss on her lips, just to show her how serious I was about all of this.

"And I don't...I mean, I know we're working together, and we need to take this case seriously," she went on. "But I was...I was thinking that maybe..."

"You want to keep doing stuff like that?" I asked. She looked up at me, teeth digging into her bottom lip.

"I guess I do," she admitted. "I haven't been with anyone else in a long time, and I think it's good for me to have someone to work out those feelings with, you know?"

"Tell me about it," I agreed, and she flashed me a smile.

"What has it been for you, two weeks?" she asked playfully. I grinned.

"Something like that," I agreed. "Feels like a lifetime, though."

"Oh, my heart just bleeds for you." She laughed, and I realized we were flirting with each other. Actually flirting. More than just the playful office banter we normally shared, something was really happening here, and I was sincerely enjoying it.

"So, tell me," I said, leaning forward and lowering my voice. "What was it you liked about what we did?"

She parted her lips in surprise, clearly not having been ready for that question, but I liked to know what got off the people I fucked – and I got the feeling that our desires were closer in line than I had ever imagined they could be.

"I guess I liked it when you..." she began, and then she caught herself, clearly not quite sure how to get the words out of her mouth without sounding like an asshole.

"You can tell me," I assured her gently. It was strange, I had never seen her shy before, but there was something totally adorable about it, something that I found totally charming. I wanted to show her she was safe with me, that she was safe to tell me anything she wanted.

"I liked it when you took control," she blurted out finally, and then she looked back up at me and chewed her lip as she waited for me to respond.

It took a second for me to wrap my head around what she was saying to me. Abi had always been the girl who was totally in control of her life, of her work, or everything that came with it. And now she was telling me she liked it when I was the one calling the shots? Interesting. Very interesting indeed...

"You did?" I asked, and she nodded.

"It felt like a...relief," she confessed. "Like a weight off my shoulders. I have to be in charge all the time around here, and I knew I didn't have to worry about that when the two of us were together. I liked it. A lot."

I could tell from the way she was speaking that she was turning herself on just with the thought of what we had done that night, and, in truth, I could feel a little stirring inside of me as she spoke.

"You want me to do that again?" I asked her, and she nodded, her cheeks darkening a little as though she could hardly believe she was saying all of this out loud to me. But I loved it. To hear her admit that she wanted me — I couldn't think of anything sexier in the world. Apart from, maybe, just maybe, seeing how far she would go to prove that she really did want me.

"How about right now?" I pressed, and she looked up at me in surprise.

"Here? In the office?" she asked, and I nodded.

"In the office," I replied. "Come here."

She rose to her feet, slowly, nervously, as though fearful of where this was going to take her and what she was going to do next. But she moved towards me, carefully, putting one foot in front of the other like she was tracing a path she had never trodden before.

"On your knees," I told her, pushing my chair back from the desk a little. She paused for an instant, and then did as she was told, sinking down to her knees before me.

God, she looked good like that. On her knees, gazing up at

me, waiting for her command. I had been with plenty of women before, but there was something about taking control of her, this woman who was usually the most powerful in the room, that turned me on more than anything I had ever experienced before in my life.

"Undo my pants," I commanded her, and she reached forward and did as she was told at once. I glanced to make sure the door was fully shut behind her, and it was, the lock pushed over, too. Hmm. So she had wanted us to have our privacy, had she? I wondered if something like this had been on her mind, too...

"Stroke it," I told her, as she slowly wrapped her hand around the length of my cock and began to, slowly, stroke with her fingers. Her hand was shaking, but I could see from the expression of sheer carnal lust on her face that she wanted this. She really meant this, huh? She hadn't just been telling me what she wanted to hear, she had been getting as much out of this as I had. And I was going to enjoy every moment of it.

"Kiss the top."

She did as she was told at once, closing her eyes and planting a soft, warm peck on the head of my cock. I groaned and tipped my head back in my seat. There was a decadence to getting blown like this that nothing could even come close to matching, and I knew this memory was going to be burned into my brain for a hell of a long time to come. Something about seeing her there, this woman I had known for so long, giving me what I wanted any way I wanted it, it was so perfect I could hardly contain myself.

"Take your time," I ordered her. "Slide your mouth down over it. The whole thing."

"I don't know if I can fit all of it..." she protested, a little worried, and I reached down and stroked her head.

"I know that you can, Abi," I told her. I had seen her do far more challenging things than taking my thick seven inches down her throat, and I had no doubt she would be able to make this work just the same way she did everything else in her life.

And, with my encouragement, she did as she was told – and sure enough, it didn't take long until she had managed to slide her mouth down around my full length. She had to take breaks to catch her breath a couple of times, but she pulled it off, her lips soon wrapped around my base, her hands on my thighs as though she was bracing herself and making sure she didn't lose her balance. I wouldn't let her. I reached down to stroke her hair, and she looked up at me, her eyes watering slightly from where my cock had caused her to catch her breath.

"You look so beautiful like that," I told her, and I could see the way her eyes lit up when I gave her that positive feedback. She might not have known it quite yet, but she was made for this. Made for kneeling between my legs, using her mouth to pleasure me as I directed her to give me what I wanted.

"Okay, up and down now," I told her, and she began to move her head, her mouth sliding the length of my cock and then down again, like she was trying to swallow me whole. Her lips were warm and wet and her fingers dug into my thighs and I knew it wouldn't be long until I came. I was sure someone was going to come in and bust the two of us in the act, but it was hard to give much of a damn when she looked so fucking good sucking my cock on her knees at my desk.

"Fuck, yes," I groaned, and I reached down to run a hand through her hair, gripping the back of her head so I could control the speed and depth of her lips on my cock. She felt incredible, looked even better, and I knew I was already forming an addiction – an addiction I was going to have a hard time breaking. She was just so *good.*

"Tell me," I said to her, and she looked up at me again, those eyes wide and almost pleading for me to give her what she wanted.

"Where do you want me to come?"

She widened her eyes at me for a moment, and I saw that pinkness return to her cheeks. I allowed her to slip her mouth off me, and then she bit her lip as she tried to come up with the words to tell me what she needed me to hear.

"I want you to come...in my mouth," she replied, and I stroked her hair softly.

"Say it louder, now," I told her gently.

"In my mouth," she told me again, her voice a little more certain this time. "I want you to come in my mouth."

"Of course, baby," I said back to her, and I guided her lips back on to my cock.

It didn't take long until I was tipping myself over the edge and into the release I needed so badly – I felt my balls begin to tingle, and sure enough, a few seconds later, I unleashed a jet of my seed into her mouth, down her throat, just like she had asked me to. She moaned softly as I came, sending a delicious rush of vibrations up through my entire body. I had to press my lips together to keep from making a noise the whole of the rest of the office would hear, and as a result, it felt as though the pleasure was turning inward, so beautiful and powerful I could hardly think straight for a second.

Gently, I reached down and pushed her back from my cock, her lips leaving my spent dick with a slight popping sound that made me smile.

"You're too good at that," I groaned to her, and she beamed up at me.

"I think I might need a little more practice yet," she replied, and she rose to her feet, smoothing down her skirt and fixing her hair. And, as I watched her try to get back to office-ready, I knew things were about to get seriously distracting around here.

8

ABIGAIL

"Shh, someone's going to catch us!" I protested, trying to keep my giggles to a minimum so we wouldn't be busted in the act. But honestly, as his lips found mine and he closed the office door behind us, I couldn't have much cared less.

It was hard to believe we had only started doing this a couple of weeks ago – I had given him that blowjob in the office, and from there on out, it had been all fun, all the time, and I didn't want to give it up for an instant. I would never have believed I would allow myself to give in to my desires in this way, but the more time that passed, the more I became certain this was just the only way to live – and the only way I was going to keep my head on straight in the stress of managing the case that Kim was bringing against him.

It made sense, really, given that he was trying to keep his head down as much as possible, keeping himself out of the clubs and everything so he didn't get busted getting up to something that might have landed him in trouble. And sure, I had been going without for so long it seemed only fair I indulge myself in a little fun, right?

I had never been with a guy like him before. Not in my

entire life. I had never been with a guy who took control so utterly, and who made me love every instant of it. I liked to think of myself as the woman who ran everything in her life, but when it came to him — when it came to him, all of that just seemed to fall away completely and utterly, and I didn't just like it, I *loved* it. I needed it. I craved it. I lay awake at night thinking of all the ways I could pleasure him, and then I came in the next day to find he had been thinking just the same thing, too.

We had put a few rules in place, to make sure we didn't do anything that would have landed us in too much trouble – we had to make sure nobody else at the office was going to find out what we were up to, and nobody outside it was to know, either. This was just between us. A chance for the both of us to blow off some steam while we were working so closely with one another, and nothing more than that.

"Maybe we should keep it out of the office entirely," I suggested, over a drink at his place after he had dragged me out of the office to hook up in the middle of the day.

"Oh, but it's so much fun there," he replied, a devilish smile flicking up his lips. I felt a flutter in my stomach. I knew he was right. It was totally filthy, but whenever I was with him in the confines of his office – bent over his desk, on my knees beside him, anything – it was as though a switch had been flicked and I could give in entirely to the desires that seemed to keep me obsessed with him.

I had always known he was a powerful guy but being with him sexually had just underlined that point past the notion of any denial. He was more than powerful – he commanded the room, commanded everything and anything inside of it. When he issued an order, I knew I had to follow it, that it would be worth my while in the long run. He always made sure of that. My rewards were equal to my tasks, and the further and further

I was willing to go for him, the more he would pay me back in return.

And, of course, amongst all of this, we still had work to think about, as well. The case Kim had brought against him was still alive and kicking. We had managed to keep it under wraps enough that other people weren't reporting on it yet, thank God, but it was only a matter of time before people started sticking their goddamn noses into what we were trying to hide.

I still hadn't been able to dig up much on Kim; I knew she came from a rich family, but there was a big-ass gap between her leaving them and her arriving to work for Karl. There had to be something she was trying to hide, something she had wiped from the record. I had tried to delve in as far as I could, but there was nothing coming up, and I knew I would have to take a different approach to shake loose what I needed to find.

"What about other names?" Karl had suggested to me. "I've only ever known her as an Isler, but there's no way she was able to wipe everything from the record just like that."

"You think she might have been married or something?" I asked, and he nodded.

"I don't know if you can get hold of marriage records in this state, but maybe you could try?" he suggested. I chewed on my lip, pissed that I hadn't thought of it.

"That's where I'll go next," I agreed. I needed to stop getting so caught up in the way I was feeling about him – I still had a job to do, and I wasn't going to go letting myself forget that anytime soon. Not a chance in hell. Not when I had just started to find the balance between the desires that made me feel like I had the release I needed, and the work I had perfected for so long.

Digging in on Kim's past was harder than it needed to be. Like she was trying to hide something. I had no idea what it was she might have been trying to keep under wraps, and frankly, I was getting more and more intrigued with every new leaf I uncovered. She had come from this rich-ass family, but they had lost a big chunk of their money in the market crash back in 2008, when she had been a teenager. Her father had become pretty much broke, and she had been left to pick up the pieces that remained after everything he had done – he fled the country with a younger woman, and she and her family had to cover his debts and everything else he had left behind. It was quite a mess for a young woman her age to deal with, the sort of thing that could have sent her spiraling down a bad path if she wasn't careful. But I had no idea if she had taken that route – and, if she had, what that path might have looked like.

I trusted Karl. Of course I did. I wouldn't have been doing any of this for him if I didn't totally believe he was innocent of everything she had accused him of. But that didn't mean I didn't find myself wondering, jealously, if something really had happened between him and this other woman. I knew it was in no way my place to go digging, but I turned up everything I could on the two of them, every time they had so much as been seen in public together, to try to shake the nerves that were taking over the back of my head.

I had never been jealous like that before. Not really. I had never honestly cared if the guys I had been fooling around with had been seeing other people, even though I knew some of them wanted me to be pissed off about it – I just didn't have it in me to give much of a damn. But with him? Yeah, with him, something was different. Maybe because we'd had something good together. Maybe because there was something real there, and I didn't like the thought of sharing it with anyone. Least of all the very person I had been tasked with digging up dirt on.

Eventually, I figured the only way I was going to get to the bottom of Kim Isler was if I did a little digging into the company that was providing her legal counsel to bring the case against us. They must have believed it was worth it, and usually, that meant they had the money to burn. But she couldn't have been paying them with her family funds, so where the hell was she getting this from, that was what I wanted to know...

I managed to get hold of the secretary from the firm, pretending with my best fake accent to be someone I wasn't, and sure enough, it didn't take me long until I had dug up something that seemed to point me in the right direction. They were the same firm, the woman blurted out to me before she could stop herself, that had dealt with Kim's claim on her deceased husband's estate, and made sure she got all the money she was due.

"And what was the name of her husband?" I asked her, feeling as though I had struck gold.

"Uh, Robert Paisley," the woman replied. "What are you calling about, again?"

"Oh, just one of Ms. Isler's representatives from the bank," I replied as vaguely and as cheerfully as I could, hoping it would be enough to sate her curiosity without giving away anything further.

"Thanks for your help," I replied quickly, and I hung up the phone before she could ask any more difficult questions about who exactly I was and what exactly I intended to do with the information I had been given. Robert Paisley, Robert Paisley – why did that name ring a bell? Where had I heard it before...?

It didn't take me long to find out what the hell was going on there. Robert Paisley had died the year before, which wouldn't have been too surprising for a man in his sixties, apart from the fact that he had gone out on one of his boats in the middle of the night and never made a return, totally out-of-character for his usually-sensible self, according to his family. The only person he had left his considerable fortune to in his will was his wife, the much-younger Kim Paisley. The two of them were pictured together in the article about him, and there was no doubt in my mind – it was her. A little younger, yes, with her hair dyed a deep brown instead of the bleached blonde it was now, but it was her.

I read a little further into the case – it had been covered pretty extensively by the media, and there was still some kind of question about what the hell had happened to him at the end-up. The family had pushed for more investigation, but when his body had turned up on a beach, drowned and practically preserved from all the alcohol pickling his organs, the cops had decided to drop it and put it down to intoxication and an accident. The Paisleys had attempted to pursue a civil suit, but that had been dropped pretty quickly, for reasons I couldn't confirm one way or the other.

A nagging feeling tugged at the back of my mind. I knew it was crazy, but – but could Kim have had something to do with what had happened to him? She hadn't bothered to keep his name, as though she was trying to move herself as far away from their relationship as she could. Which might have been the natural reaction of a grieving spouse trying to get on with their lives, or else an admission of something she didn't want to have to remember if she could avoid it.

I needed to know more, and it didn't take long for me to go deep-diving into everything I could find about her relationship with Robert. The two of them had only been married a couple of years when he died, and even when they had gotten married, there had been a few raised eyebrows in the local press. He was the son of an oil tycoon, and she was some one-time heiress who looked to be digging for gold as much as his father had been digging for oil.

But that wasn't the only interesting thing about their union. No, it was the fact that when their wedding was reported on, it was covered with both their names – Robert Paisley and Kim Desorano. Which was pretty far removed from her maiden name of Isler, right?

I felt like I was tumbling down a rabbit hole, unable to stop, as I uncovered more about that name and how she had come to call it her own. I wondered how much she had paid her lawyers to get this shit off the Internet, because it seemed like every two minutes I hit another dead-end. What was she trying to hide? Why did she have that name? What was going on...?

"Hey."

A voice caught my attention, and I looked up to see Karl leaning in the doorway, looking down at me with a smile on his face. I managed to return it, even though it felt like my brain was too busy to focus on anything in that moment.

"You alright?" he asked me, and I managed to nod.

"It's just been a long day, that's all," I replied. I wasn't going to tell him anything, I resolved, until I had the full story. I didn't know how long it would take to find it, but those were the rules I was making for myself.

"Let's see if I can get you to forget all about it, huh?" he suggested playfully, and I knew I couldn't handle this level of flirting at the office without combusting on the spot.

"Sure," I replied, trying to keep my voice casual as I went to grab my coat and rose to my feet. "My place?"

"Your place," he agreed, and the glint in his eyes told me he had a whole lot planned for as soon as he got me all to himself once more.

And I was looking forward to forgetting about work for a while. Because whatever was going on with Kim Isler – or whatever the hell name she was using for herself these days – I knew it was something seriously questionable. And I was going to do everything I could to make sure I uncovered the truth, before she made a permanent mess of the life of the man I just couldn't get enough of right now.

9

KARL

I locked eyes with Abigail across the table and tried to make sense of what she had just said to me.

"You're telling me," I repeated after her, speaking slowly, making sure I had heard all of this right. "That she...that she was married twice before she came to work for me?"

"Yeah, that's right," she agreed, grimacing and shaking her head. "I didn't think she would be able to sneak both of those off her record but seems like she's been doing her best to keep that under wraps."

"I can't believe I didn't hear anything about this," I said, shaking my head, sure there must have been something I was missing. Yes, okay, I might not have been the most attentive guy in the world when it came to society weddings, but I thought I would have heard about the strange circumstances that had surrounded at least her last breakup. Or, indeed, the breakup of the boat of the man she had said she loved.

"So what happened to the first one?" I asked her. "You told me about Robert Paisley, I think I follow that one. What about the first guy?"

"Donald Ilerson," she told me, pulling out a file from her

bag. She had been working her ass off on this for the last week or so, and had promised to come to me when she had it all in hand, when she had everything worked out and knew just what she wanted to do and everything she wanted to tell me.

"The two of them got married when she was twenty," she explained. "Even then, people thought that it was weird."

"Yeah, well, that's because it is," I agreed, and she nodded.

"She didn't think so," she replied. "She made a big stink about how people were judging them and didn't understand anything they had together. It was...strange, to say the least. I couldn't find much about it, but there's enough to see she wanted everyone to know she was taking this seriously."

"Like she had something to prove?" I asked, and she nodded.

"Like she had something to prove," she agreed. "I still can't believe how much of a fuss she was making about it – like she didn't want anyone to forget she was the one who had gotten him, even though apparently she wasn't the only one after him."

"And what happened to him at the end of all of that?" I asked with interest. "She must have gotten rid of him somehow, if she went on to marry that other dude."

"It seems like she was just as unlucky with him as she was with her second husband," she replied, a tinge of sarcasm to her voice, and I could tell she didn't believe a word of whatever it was that Kim had put out there hoping the rest of the world would believe.

"Why, what happened to him?"

"He was killed in a car accident," she explained. "But here's the thing – he was one of the best drivers any of his friends or family knew. He used to race part-time, and this wasn't another driver being shitty, this was him apparently just swerving right off the road and into a ditch and dying on impact, even though his car had been modded with special safety equipment for his racing."

"Shit," I said, as she pushed across the table towards me a newspaper article covering the news of Donald's sudden death. The car in the picture was a mangled wreck, and it didn't take much to see he wouldn't have made it out of there alive.

"And you think she had something to do with this?" I asked her, looking back up at her once more. If there was anyone I trusted with all of this, then it would have been her, but I still couldn't believe easily that all of this had just happened without any suspicion falling on her.

"I'm certain she did," she replied. "She's gone after two rich guys, both of whom died really out-of-character deaths in remote places and left her a whole fuck-ton of money after they passed. That strikes me as a little strange, wouldn't you agree?"

"I sure as hell would," I remarked, shaking my head. "But why would she do this?"

"Her family was rich as hell when she was growing up," Abigail replied. "But they lost most of their money back in '08, when the market crashed. I think she's trying to get back on top with all of that, so she can live the kind of life she got used to when she was a kid. Just speculation, but with so little out there about her, it's not as though I can do much more than that."

I leaned back in my seat for a moment, taking in everything she had said to me. It just didn't seem as though it could be real. But what she had laid out for me, it was hard to deny. The facts were there, and they seemed to point in one direction and one direction alone.

"And what do you think this means for the case?" I asked. "The one that she brought against me, I mean. You make a pretty compelling case for everything that happened with her husbands, but I'm not sure how it ties into everything that happened with me."

"Obviously, without spending more time with her or figuring out exactly what she wanted from the case," she replied, furrowing her brow, "I think I would guess she was planning to use you to get more money. It's been a few years since her husband died, and it wouldn't surprise me if she'd run out of money already."

"And what, you think she might have been trying to get me to hand it over to her or something?"

"I think so," she agreed, with a sigh. "Maybe she thought you were going to settle down with her and get married. And then, if something happened to you..."

"Then that would just be bad luck," I said, and she nodded.

"Something like that," she agreed. I felt a cold shiver run down my spine. I would never have fallen for someone like her, not in a million years – Kim was too cold, too calculating, too fake. But the thought that she might have had those designs on me in the first place was enough to get me feeling all sticky around the edges.

"And I would guess this case she's bringing against you now is a way for her to get the money from you she wanted in the first place," she finished up. "That would explain why she offered you the chance to just pay her off and make it go away. She was most likely hoping for that option, and now that you've turned her down..."

She trailed off, let out a long sigh.

"I don't know what she's going to do now," she admitted. I reached across the table and took her hand, squeezing tight. It was the sort of gesture of affection we normally tried to avoid at the office, but I couldn't just sit there, looking at the expression on her face, and not want to do something to help.

"It's going to be alright," I promised her. I hoped she believed me. I knew how hard it could be to accept the help you needed, even when the person offering it to you wanted you to take it more than anything. It wasn't fair to her that she'd had to carry all this weight alone – she had dug up something that could have major implications, and I was going to make sure she didn't have to drag all that around alone any longer.

"I hope so," she admitted. "I just don't know what I'm going to do with all of this now that I know it. If she hasn't been caught by now, then I don't know how we're going to use any of this to prove that she's...that she's something *wrong*."

The way she said that word, with such vitriol, told me she meant this. She wanted this to be over as much as I did. And I was sure there was something to it, something more than just her job. Like me, she wanted to put this behind us so the two of us could just be together. No complications. This case might have brought us together, but as soon as it was done with, we would be able to see what the two of us looked like on the other side of that.

I had no idea what that was going to look like, but maybe it was alright. Maybe I didn't have to know, not yet. Maybe it was fine for the two of us to just figure this out as we went along, and whatever happened, would happen.

"I think we should take this to court," she told me, finally, narrowing her eyes and hitting me with a determined look.

"How long will that take?"

"I have no idea," she admitted. "But I know we can prove she's got a pattern with the rich men in her life, and when people realize that, she's never going to have the power in this town she did before."

"That sounds like a plan to me," I remarked, and she smiled at me, finally, her face lighting up. That was enough to make me grin back at her. Seeing her happy, that was all I needed to make me feel alive in a way I never had before.

"Then we're going to take her on," she replied. And, judging by the certainty in her voice, I knew that, as long as I had her on my side, we would win.

10

ABIGAIL

"No shit," I said, as soon as I got to the email in my inbox. "*No shit.*"

Of all the ways I thought this would turn out, this was about the last one on the list. I had gone to Kim's lawyers to let them know our intention of taking her to court to contest the charges she had laid in front of us, and they had hung up on me – refusing to give away any strategy, I had assumed. Until an email pinged into my messages and told me we might just have already won.

They were giving in. They had dropped Kim as a client, and they were making it about as clear as they could they didn't want anything more to do with her case. What had they found out about her? I was itching to email them back and find out, but I knew they wouldn't have said anything anyway – I would have to just keep on guessing.

I read the email three times over before I convinced myself that it was real and it wasn't something I was just making up because I wanted this to be over. I was sure I had to be going crazy, but no – this was actually happening, they had really gotten rid of her, and without representation, she was going to have a damn hard time fighting this case, wasn't she?

Not to mention the fact she would have a hard time tracking down new representation now she had been shifted from her current lawyers. Nobody wanted to pick up the case of a person who had behaved badly enough to get tossed from a previous lawyer. No doubt whatever reason they had given her would soon be spread around the industry; it would get back to me, sooner or later. But for now, it was done. Over. And Kim Isler, for whatever reason she had gone after Karl in the first place, had dropped the case.

I made sure to send the news to a couple of industry news sites who had been keeping track of the story, and, as soon as those emails were off into cyberspace, I sat back in my seat and gazed at the ceiling and felt a huge grin spreading across my face. *Yes.* Yes, okay, finally. It was over. I had been right to trust Karl all along, and, now that it was done with, now that it was behind us, I could figure out what the hell came next for the two of us.

Shit. I hadn't even really thought about what happened after this. When we had been working together on this, we had been aligned on our goals, only one thing in both of our minds – proving this case had no grounding and getting him off the hook. And now it was done...well, what now?

I was involved with Karl. I was actually involved with him. Something I had told myself I was never going to do, something I had promised myself I would never have fallen for, no matter how much I might have wanted to.

He had only been holding off on going out and picking up women on my advice, because it would have looked bad for his case. But that didn't mean we didn't have something, right? It was more than just sex, it was something else at this point, something that ran a little deeper than that, something that was more than just him putting his dick inside of me. We had chemistry. Intense chemistry. Or did he have that with every woman he slept with?

Fucking hell. Where did all of this insecurity come from? I was confident in myself, or at least, I had been before I found myself falling for this guy. I just knew there was so much competition out there, so many women in the city who had a history with him just the same way I did – so many who wanted him just the same way I did, too. They might have tried to deny it, but I knew the truth. I knew how they saw him. And now he was back on the market...

I rubbed my hands over my face and let out a long sigh. This wasn't who I was. This was never who I had been. I wanted to get the rush of distress out of my head, the sadness, the second-guessing. I was confident in everything about myself, but when it came to him, it felt like the confidence just started to leak out of me as though it had never been there in the first place.

But he had done nothing but give me what I wanted. Over and over again. Made me come, made me squirm, made me want him even more and more. And now I had to figure out what the hell the two of us looked like now that we were out of the woods, and into something – into something else entirely.

I texted him to let him know about the retraction of the accusations, and, at once, he suggested heading out for dinner to celebrate – as colleagues? As friends? As something more? I had no clue, and no idea if I should ask him or not. I would just have to see where he took me and base it off that. Yes. That made sense. I could manage that. Couldn't I?

I went home to change into something that looked a little more date-appropriate – no idea if I was actually going on one or not, but I wanted to be ready if the answer was yes. I changed my outfit at least three times before I settled on something that even remotely looked the way I wanted to look. I needed to show him I was worth more than just the hook-ups we'd been having while we had been working on this project together. Though I wouldn't have been surprised if he had been heading out there to find a couple of women to burn off his excess sexual energy with already. Now that he didn't have this case to worry about, why should he have bothered to hold back or hide out from his true desires? Why should he have settled for someone like me?

He texted me the name of the restaurant he wanted to go to, and I promised myself I wasn't going to look it up to try to get a better feel of what he wanted from me in the first place. I was just going to turn up and act like anything that happened was what I had been expecting from the start. And try my very best to put to the back of my mind the fact he was my boss, and he had made me come harder than anyone had in my entire life before I had met him.

By the time I headed down to the meeting spot, I could feel the nerves racing through me, demanding my attention, my brain rushing overtime as it tried to make sense of everything that was coursing through my mind. I hated this. I hated how much I couldn't seem to chill myself out. And I hated that some part of me, deep in the back of my mind, wanted this case to keep going, because then he wouldn't have been able to go out into the world and pick up all the women he wanted all over again. I hated that most of all. And I wasn't going to let that part of me run the show.

He was already there when I arrived, and he was wearing a navy suit with darker stripes that made him look even more handsome than normal. My heart loop-the-looped inside my chest, and I tried my best to keep my face neutral and chill, hoping all the tension inside of me wasn't showing on my face.

He greeted me with a kiss on the cheek, the scent of his aftershave rushing up to fill my senses, and when he pulled back, I could feel my knees getting a little week underneath me.

"I can't believe it's finally over," he remarked, his voice giddy with the thrill of everything that had happened.

"Yeah, she dropped it so quickly," I agreed. "Or the company did, rather. I doubt they're going to be taking her on for another case anytime soon."

"And that's all that matters," Karl agreed, pulling out a chair for me so I could sit down; such a gentleman. I felt a little flutter in my guts as I tried to soothe my overthinking brain. I couldn't stop wondering just what it was he wanted from me.

"Do you think it's really all over?" he asked, as he waved over the waiter and asked for a bottle of wine; he didn't bother to stop and think about what I might have wanted, but I didn't mind that. Because he already knew damn well. He knew me well enough that he didn't have to second-guess. And that was one of the things I liked most about him.

"I think so," I agreed. "I can't see how she'd make another approach on this. If it's about making more money, then I don't think she'd want to spend any more than she already has. She's already looking at losing a good stack of cash, I doubt she's going to be in any hurry to do it all over again."

"Damn, that's good to hear," he said, shaking his head and grinning widely. "You know how long I've been waiting to hear that?"

"As long as I have," I replied, as the waiter returned with the wine; Karl tasted it, and then nodded for it to be poured into my glass. I watched as the deep red liquid filled up the glass in front of me and wondered why it was that there was something so soothing to me about the way he seemed to take control. I loved it about him, his sureness, his confidence – he never seemed to second-guess what he was doing, or have to check in with me. He just knew what he wanted, and that was, as far as he was concerned, the only thing that really mattered. And I sure as hell wasn't going to let myself get caught complaining about it.

The food was perfect, and he had his hand on my knee under the table the entire time, a promise that perhaps this really was the date I had hoped it would be. His touch was enough to make me giddy and needy, and I was having a hard time focusing on everything he was saying, as the wine and the desire got me intoxicated, too drunk on him to think properly.

As the night wore on, I could see him looking at me with the naked want that told me just what was on his mind. I didn't even know how to put it into words, but it was enough to make everything feel a little easier. A little more straightforward. He wanted me, and that was all that I cared about, and I intended to make the very most of it I could while I was still able to. I had no idea what was going to come after this evening was over, but for now, I had him all to myself, and that was the only thing in the damn world that mattered to me.

"There's something I want to ask you," he said to me, voice low, eyes soft. My heart skipped a beat. Was he going to say it? Was he going to ask me to make this official? I had no idea, no idea if that's even what I really wanted, but I had to hear him out. I leaned forward, closing the distance between us, and looking him dead in the eye as I nodded back at him.

"Anything," I replied, and a smile spread over his face, eyes flashing with a deviant glint that told me everything I needed to know. Moving his mouth towards my ear, and keeping his voice soft, he spoke the words I hadn't expected to hear – but that I needed to more than anything right now.

"Go wait for me in the bathroom," he told me. "Take off your panties. And don't move a muscle until I'm in there with you."

11

KARL

I counted down the seconds until I could follow her away from the table, hoping I had left a good enough tip with the waiter to be able to get away with this without attracting too much attention. I had a grin on my face half a mile wide, and I could hardly wait to get my hands on her again. But for now, I would wait as long as it took to make sure nobody caught on to what we were doing together – because waiting just made it all the sweeter, right?

I couldn't believe the case with Kim was finally over and done with. Hard to believe, really, that it had been that easy all along, but thank goodness, it was over. And I knew I had Abi to thank for it. And I intended to make sure I thanked her in a way that she would never be able to forget, that was for damn sure...

I avoided the gaze of the waiter, who was probably wondering where Abi had gone to, and waited long enough that I was sure nobody would catch on to what we were doing together. I had fooled around in public plenty of times with plenty of women, but there was something about asking Abigail to do this for me that turned me on more than anything in the world.

I knew it was her power. Her power aroused me more than anything else. And knowing she was so willing to just hand that power over to me every chance she got, as long as it made me happy. The women I had been with before, they hadn't had the status to give away, but Abi? Abi did, and she seemed willing to hand it over to me every single time I so much as hinted in that direction.

I rose to my feet, trying to keep my face neutral, and followed her to the large unisex bathroom at the back of the restaurant. I would have been lying if I'd said I hadn't picked this place with that in mind.

The door was open when I got there, and I snuck a look around before I stepped inside, not much caring if anyone saw, but wanting to be certain nobody was going to try to catch us out. And there she was, waiting for me – this woman I couldn't get enough of.

"Fuck, Abi," I groaned, as I grabbed her by the hips and pulled her in close to me, kissing her hard, pushing my tongue into her mouth as I reached to do up the lock behind me. I wouldn't have cared if someone had walked right in on the two of us in the act – frankly, I would have been glad for the chance to show her off, because I felt like I wanted most everyone to know about just how badly I wanted her. Just how crazy she drove me. Just how much I wanted to take a bite out of her every chance that I got, like she was a piece of ripe fruit, begging for my teeth against her flesh.

I didn't know how long we had, so I pushed my hand between her thighs and guided it against her pussy, finding it gratifyingly bare, just like I had told her.

"Where did you put your panties?" I asked her, and she reached into her pocket to hand them back to me. They were already a little wet, as though she had been waiting for this all night long. The thought of her needing me was enough to get me totally hard, and I knew I wasn't going to be able to hold back for another second.

"Turn around," I ordered her, spinning her so she had to catch hold of the rail on the wall to stay upright. I pulled the condom I had stashed in my pocket out, and reached around to push the panties she had just handed me into her mouth so I could keep her quiet, keep her from making too much noise and letting anyone else in this place know what we were getting up to. She let out a little squeal of surprise, muffled by the fabric, but she didn't protest. I rubbed my fingers along the outside of her slit, feeling her wetness, making sure she really wanted me as I sheathed myself quickly.

"Spread your legs," I ordered her, and she did as she was told at once – I wasn't going to wait any longer, not risking wasting another second of time. I took myself by the base and guided my dick against her pussy, sliding into her in one swift motion and feeling the welcoming warmth of her slit around me for the first time in what felt like way too long.

"Oh, fuck," I groaned, and I grabbed her hips so I could push into her even harder. The sound of her moan, even muffled by her panties, stirred something inside of me, and I knew I couldn't hold back for another second. I pushed in hard, harder, filling her roughly, going in as deep as I could over and over again, the noise of our flesh coming together the only thing filling the small space around us. Her back was arched and she was using her grasp on the rail before her to grind back against me like it was the only thing that mattered, her ass twisting this way and that as though she was pleading for as much of me as she could take.

And I was going to give that to her. I could hardly control myself as I thrust into her, over and over again – what was it about this woman that made me feel like I was losing my mind?

It was as though everything else just fell away, failed to matter as soon as I pushed inside of her. This was the high I had been craving when I had been with other girls, this was the passionate need I had wanted but never quite been able to find. And I knew that now it had started I would never be able to stop.

It wasn't long until I could feel my balls tingling, and I knew I needed to find that release before too long – I didn't know how long this place would give us before they came in and busted us, quite rightfully, in the act, and frankly, I wasn't much interested in finding out. I reached around so I could play with her clit as I pushed into her, determined to get her where she needed to go too. I could see that misty look in her eyes, the one that told me she had long since detached from the real world and was giving herself over to the pleasure I was gifting her. I loved seeing her like that. Hopeless. Helpless before anything other than what I would allow her to feel.

Sure enough, it didn't take long until I watched her come hard around my cock – her whole body spasmed, and I had to reach down and wrap my arms around her to keep her from collapsing right there on the spot. I held her close as I felt her tighten around me, and a moment or two later, I found my own release buried deep down inside of her, coming hard and filling her with my seed.

I pulled out of her quickly and reached around to hook the panties out of her mouth with my fingers, and then kissed her hard once more. She wound her arms around me, still half-undressed, letting out these hopeless little mewling noises against my mouth as though she was begging for just a little more, just a little more...

I pulled back and looked at her, her cheeks still flushed from what we had just been doing, and I couldn't help but smile. I felt a rush of affection for this woman, this woman I had known for so long but who I had just started to see in full color these last few weeks. And, before I could stop myself, I had said it.

"I love you."

12

ABIGAIL

I LAY THERE IN BED, STARING AT THE CEILING ABOVE ME, AND running the words around and around in my head, over and over again, until they had stopped making anything that even resembled sense anymore.

I love you. I love you. I love you. I love you. I love you.

There was something about the way they sounded when they had come out of his mouth that didn't make sense to me. Almost dissonant. I had never heard him speak like that before, with such softness and such care. And it made my head spin to think it had been aimed at me.

I almost felt greedy for wanting to hear it again. And again, and again, and again, until I actually believed he meant to say it and he hadn't just let it fall from his lips like it was nothing. We had just finished having sex, and I was sure the rush of emotion and endorphins that came after something like that was a better explanation for the declaration than anything else too extreme. Perhaps I was just letting myself read too much into it. I should have been more careful, more reticent with the way that I felt.

I hadn't said it back to him. I had been so damn shocked that

I'd had no idea what the hell I was meant to come out with in response to something like that. I was flattered, yes, of course I was, but that was different than believing he actually meant it. He had just blurted it out because he was drunk and happy and knew I had something to do with it, not because of anything that actually mattered.

Right?

I tossed and turned in bed that night, thinking about him. I had stood there in the bathroom after he had dropped those words on me, no idea what I was meant to do or say in response to them, hoping this might just blink out of existence so we could go back to dinner and get back to reality once again.

But instead, he had called me a car and let me head home by myself. If I had said it back to him, I was sure I would be lying in his arms in his apartment right now, not worrying about anything but having to get up for work the next day and wondering if I might have a hangover or not. I could have made it right, but I didn't, because I had no idea how the hell I was going to do that.

I didn't know if I felt the same way about him. I liked him, yes, maybe even more than that. And the sex was beyond incredible, there was no arguing with that much. But there was something...I don't know, something that scared me about letting myself fall for him properly. Because I knew how many other women had been in my exact situation, and how many of them had wound up nursing broken hearts because they hadn't been able to protect themselves in the face of his outrageous charm.

I had promised myself the first day I'd met him I wasn't going to let it happen to me. I wasn't going to allow myself to fall for him, no matter how handsome he was, no matter how charming, no matter how sweet. But in the time that had passed, I had allowed myself to forget all the rules I had put in place for myself, all the goals I had set, because he was just – ugh. He was just more than I could control myself around. It felt like I was going crazy when I was around him, in the best way possible, as though something had come unhinged at the back of my mind and allowed me to forget all the good sense I had spent years trying to pull together in the first place.

What did he want from me? I wasn't sure, and I wasn't sure I had the good sense to just come out and ask him, either. What if he thought it was a mistake, telling me he felt that way about me? What if he was already cursing the slip of the tongue, and would tell me first thing tomorrow, when I came into the office, that he hadn't meant it and we should just put that whole thing behind us? The pain that stabbed into my heart when I considered that outcome should have been enough to tell me there was still something that passed for feeling for him burning down in my guts, but I had no idea how to come close to putting it into words right now...

Ugh. I rolled out of bed, dropping the covers on the floor, and went to switch on the A/C. It was boiling in here, or maybe it was just the heat of my blood rushing around my body that was making me feel this way. I could almost make out the sensation of his fingers against my skin. I could almost remember how good it felt to have him kiss me, to have him take control of me like that. To know he could have had any woman in this city he wanted, and he would still come back to me, that I was still what he desired above all else...

It was still far too fucking hot in here for my liking. I went to flip the window open to let in some cool air from the city outside; I tossed the window away from the latch and let the rush of coolness flood through me. Closing my eyes, and leaning on the window frame, I inhaled a big lungful of fresh air. Okay, I was starting to feel a little better now, even though I knew there was still a hell of a lot for me to figure out before I should really start to feel okay once more.

Down on the street below, I heard a noise pierce the quiet. I opened my eyes and narrowed my gaze, trying to see what was going on down there. It had to be three in the morning, and this place was usually pretty quiet, filled with people who had to head to their offices first thing in the morning and who didn't want to be up late if they could avoid it. Myself included, though I had already committed to running on coffee for the rest of the day if I had to.

And then, I saw it. A woman. Sliding quickly into a car, as though she didn't want to be seen. I peered down to try to get a better look at her, but she was gone before I could make her out properly, the pool of light from the streetlamp beside the car she had just climbed into an icy yellow on the ground below. Normally, I would have just brushed it off without a second thought, but I was sure I recognized the woman. I just couldn't place where it was I happened to know her...

And before I could ponder it any further, the car she had climbed into whipped off down the street, the sound of the engine and the screeching tires filling the air. Whoever was there, they didn't want to be in this place for another second.

I felt a shiver run down my spine. Something was wrong. I was sure of it. There was something about the way the woman had moved and the speed at which the car had gotten out of here that made me feel like I was going to throw up. I didn't like this, not one bit, and I reached for my phone, closing my fingers around it before I could stop myself...

But who the hell was I going to call? The police? What, and tell them I had seen someone driving out of here pretty fast with a woman in the car who had probably served me coffee sometime, or something? Yeah, that would just go down like a charm. I was being crazy, and I needed to pull my shit together if I was going to find some way to face what was going on in my life right now.

I let go of my phone, and slipped back into bed, letting the covers lie on the floor beside me. I was too hot. I needed to cool off. And, more than anything, I needed to work out what the hell I was going to do about seeing Karl the next day. And if I felt the same way about him that he claimed to feel about me.

13

KARL

I drummed my fingers on the table in front of me as I waited for her to arrive. I had no idea what I was going to say to her, but I was certain I needed to come out with something if I was going to convince her not to quit on the spot over my being a clingy bastard when the two of us had just been having a good time.

I had no idea how she really felt about everything that had happened the night before. I'd paid the bill, called her a cab, and she had been out of there before I'd had a chance to ask her anything more pointed. I just wanted her to know how I felt, but now I was sure I had managed to grossly overstep the line, and I just had to wait for her to arrive at work and hope I could walk things back far enough that she wouldn't call things off on the spot.

"You wanted to see me?"

A familiar voice drew my attention, and I looked up to see Abi standing in the doorway of the office; she looked nervous, dark rings under her eyes as though she had been tossing and turning all night long. You and me both, Abi.

"Yeah, I did," I replied, and I pushed the coffee I had picked up for her across the table, a peace offering. "And don't worry, I'm not going to declare my love for you again."

She managed a smile, even though it was a slightly nervous one, and she planted herself down in the seat opposite me and took a sip of the coffee I had brought for her.

"So," she began. "I guess we need to talk about it, don't we?"

"I guess we do," I agreed, and I winced as I tried to work out where I was even meant to begin with putting all of this together. There was so much I wanted to say to her, and most of it revolved around the word *sorry* for dumping such a giant declaration on her with no warning.

"Thanks for the coffee," she told me, with a little smile.

"Yeah, well, I thought you could use it, after all the wine we had last night..."

"Was that why you...was it because of the wine? That you said that?" she asked me. She was trying to keep her voice light and failing totally. I could tell she would have been hurt if I'd said yes. I shook my head at once.

"No, it wasn't because of that," I replied. "I see why you could think that way, but I...I meant it. I think."

"You only think?" she asked, and she burst out laughing. "Okay, I don't think that's what every girl dreams of hearing in response to that..."

"I haven't said it in so long, I guess I just forgot what it felt like to really mean it," I confessed. "But I do. Mean it, I mean. With you. I wanted you to hear it from me, I wanted you to know that's how I felt about you."

Her face softened slightly, and I could tell I had managed to make an impact, even though I wasn't quite sure how.

"I'm just sorry I sprung it on you out of nowhere," I explained. "That's what I wanted to tell you. And I totally get it if it's too soon for you; we don't have to jump into anything, I'm in no rush..."

"You really love me?" she asked me, her voice small, and I nodded.

"Of course I do," I replied. "Why wouldn't I?"

She shook her head, and for a moment, she gazed off into space, as though trying to find the words to give me the answer I needed.

"Because you could have anyone in this city you wanted," she pointed out. "Any woman at all. Don't pretend like you couldn't. I know you have a line out the door waiting to do anything you want if you snapped your fingers."

"So what?"

"So why me?" she asked. "Why would you choose me when you could have anyone you wanted? That's what I want to know. That's what it's going to take for me to believe you."

"Because..." I trailed off. I didn't know what to say to her. My feelings for her were so obvious to me that I had never thought to try to put them into words, and the thought of having to find some way to verbalize what I just knew to be true was almost impossible for me to wrap my head around.

"Because you're the only person who moves in the same world as me, who gets it," I replied. "You're the only one who sees me for who I am. All of me. Not just the parts of me you want or that you want something out of."

She smiled, a small smile, but a smile nonetheless. I was getting somewhere. I just had to keep talking and hope I could come out with the right thing at the right time and convince her she was the only woman I gave a damn about right now.

"The sex is a part of it, sure," I continued. "But that's just what I needed to let me see this part of you that had been here all along. It feels like...it feels like you're my other half. Like you were meant to balance me out. And I know I can't make you feel the same way about me, but I know the way I feel about you isn't going to go away anytime soon."

I caught my breath, and I looked at her, waiting for some kind of response. And, sure enough, it didn't take long until I got it. The smile that spread over her face seemed half a mile wide, and she looked down at her coffee for a moment as though contemplating everything I had just said to her.

"You really mean it?" she asked.

"I really mean it," I replied. "I mean all of it. I know this is a lot for you to take in, and you don't need to come up with an answer for me. But I love you. I want to be with you. And honestly, I think I owe Kim a thank you note, because I wouldn't have been able to see it if it wasn't for this damn case."

"I don't know what to say," she confessed, and I reached over the desk and took her hand.

"You don't have to say anything," I promised her. "I know this is a lot to take in. You don't have to have anything to say to me right now, don't worry about it. As long as you know I love you, and I'm not going anywhere, that's all I want you to know."

She gazed at me for a moment, and, for a split second, I thought I saw the hint of tears in her eyes. I had never seen her cry, in all the time I had known her, and I felt a little guilty for putting them there. But I knew they were a representation of something good, not something bad. That she finally had begun to understand I really meant what I was saying to her right now. This wasn't some sort of game, some sort of play to get her where I wanted her. This was just the way I felt, and nothing was going to stop me telling her that every single way I could.

"I don't know if I'm ready to say it back yet," she warned me. "You think you've been out of the game for a while, well, I've probably got you beat on that."

"I think we can compare notes on that later," I agreed, and she rose to her feet and came around my side of the desk so she could join me. I tugged her into my lap, and she wound her arms around my neck and gazed at me for a moment. I locked my fingers behind the small of her back, holding her still, keeping her safe.

"But I want to give this a try," she confessed. "I don't know what it looks like, I don't know what happens now, but I want to give this a try."

"That's all I needed to hear," I replied, and I pressed my lips to hers, just softly, a kiss that told her I was in no rush to get anything out of her she wasn't ready to give. When I pulled back, she had this big-ass smile on her face, almost goofy.

"You know, I'm only doing this so I can keep you out of trouble," she remarked.

"So you don't have to worry about any other cases like Kim's?" I joked back. She nodded.

"Something like that," she agreed. "Though, who knows, if I don't like the way this turns out…"

"Then I could be in trouble again," I laughed, and she nodded and planted a kiss on the corner of my mouth. I kissed her back, properly this time, letting my tongue trace the inside of her lips and smoothing my back down until it was almost cupping her ass.

"How long do you have before your next meeting?" she asked me playfully, nuzzling against my neck.

"I think they can wait a little for me," I replied, and I kissed her harder, pulling her against her, letting her feel the need for her that was already starting to swell between my legs. And I knew this was exactly how things were meant to be. This might not have been how I pictured it with her, but this was right. And that was, I decided, all I gave a damn about right now.

14

ABIGAIL

I filed away the last of the papers for the day, and checked my watch for what had to be the hundredth time since I had arrived at the office. Only an hour until I would be out of here with Karl, and that was all I could think about right now.

His name had been playing in my head since I arrived at work that day. And not in the strictly professional sense. No, in all the time we had been together, we had tried to keep our personal lives and our professional ones as far removed as possible, worried about them getting piled up on one another and turning into a huge mess. But that didn't mean I had an easy time staying focused on what I was meant to be doing, when he had been sexting me all day long and teasing me about what we were going to get up to on our date as soon as he got me out of the office.

It was hard to believe we had only been doing this for a few weeks now. We had fit this into our lives so easily it was hard to remember, sometimes, that this wasn't the way things had been since this whole thing had started in the first place. I loved having him around, loved being able to just hit him up and tease him all day and know he was sitting up there in his office and waiting for me to come down and give him what he wanted.

And the time we spent together outside of sex, too, that was the best part. He was so much fun to be around, sometimes it was hard to remember he was meant to be my boss – he always had the cutest date ideas, whisking me off to parks for ice cream in the middle of the night when I said I was craving it. I had never been with someone as spontaneous as him, and it seemed like he was working out all his impulsive needs on showing off on dates with me. Not that I was complaining. I had never been spoiled like that in my life before, and there was something impossibly sexy to me about knowing I could just let go of the reins and allow someone else to take control as soon as I was out of the office.

The balance was just so totally perfect that it sometimes felt strange I hadn't thought of it before. When I came to work, I clicked into my normal mode, the one that demanded I keep my head in the game and make sure everything gets taken care of the way it needs to be. And then, when I get off work, I get to be with someone who is totally in control, totally in charge, someone who likes nothing better than to sweep me off my feet. I could swear it was making my work more productive, too, because I was more focused knowing I would be able to switch off at the end of the day. No sitting around fretting over work emails now, not when I had someone who made me feel like I could just let go and focus on the fun stuff.

I hadn't told anyone about the two of us yet, and that was just the way I wanted to keep it. I knew a few people around the office had started to gossip about what we had been up to, and a couple of them had dropped some pointed questions my way, but it was hard to give a damn when I was having so much fun. In fact, some part of me wanted nothing more than to just tell them that yes, we were together, and we were having an amazing time, and would they like to hear the details of all the ways he made me come last night? Because I needed to talk to someone about how amazing things were between us, and I felt like keeping it in would get me all clogged up.

He had been taking me out to dinner every Friday night, and that was what I was looking forward to this evening. It had become our tradition – he would choose a restaurant, and the two of us would head out there together and have a good time and then maybe, just maybe, sneak off into the bathroom to hook up and hope the waiter didn't call us out before we were done. It was so much fun, even though it was so far removed from what I had known before; I would never have imagined, even a few months ago, that I could have public sex and enjoy it, but these days, I found myself craving it more than anything, knowing we could be caught, hell, maybe even hoping we were going to be busted in the act. I loved being with him in that way, though I would never have believed it was possible.

But my desires had morphed and changed since he had come into my life, the needs I had pushed down for so long taking control now they finally had space to breathe. I wasn't going to push them down any longer. It made me feel bold in ways I never had before, bold enough to ask for what I wanted, bold enough to demand what I needed, whether it was at work or in my personal life. I had control now, even though I often chose to hand it over to someone else. But I needed to have a hold on it in the first place for me to be able to gift it to him, right?

The only thing that was nagging at the back of my mind was what had happened the night before. I hadn't thought about the strange car and the woman scrambling in to it since the night it had happened, before we had made things official, but yesterday, when I had been heading back from my nightly run, I had spotted a car that had made my head whip around for a second look.

It was the same car as on that night. I was sure of it. I narrowed my eyes, getting a closer look at it, trying to work out if I was seeing what I actually thought I was seeing. And, sure enough, there it was – the car I had seen from my window, the one the woman had leapt into, the one that had sent the sound of those screeching tires through the street as it tore away to get as far removed from me as it possibly could.

This time, I could see the windows were tinted a dark color that blocked me from making out who was on the other side of the glass; if I had recognized the woman before, then she was making damn sure I didn't now, and there had to be a reason for that. I felt a nagging of paranoia at the back of my mind, tried to tell myself to calm the fuck down, but as I walked back towards my building, the car crawled along the pavement just behind me.

Eyes forward. Don't acknowledge they're there. I felt my heart pounding in my chest as I reached into the pocket of my leggings for my keys. Every movement I made felt unnatural. I could see the car, a bright silver, out of the corner of my eye, and I knew something strange was going on. I just had to work out what it was before they got too close...

I unlocked the door to my apartment building and closed it tight behind me, making sure the lock had clicked back into the latch before I turned to walk up the stairs. My feet carried me quickly, even though I was exhausted from my run, and before I knew it, I was back in my apartment, the door slammed behind me, feeling my heart pounding double-time in my chest as I tried to cool myself off.

Okay, okay, okay. Sometimes, strange stuff happened in this city. That didn't mean somebody was out to get me. I had nothing to worry about. I was just freaking out over nothing. It probably wasn't even the same car I had seen before, I was just getting up in my head and letting the adrenalin from my run convince me there was something bad happening when there was nothing of the sort...

I peered out of my window as soon as I was back in my apartment, and sure enough, the car was still sitting there outside my place. I had never seen it there before that first night, and I couldn't help but feel that rush of creeping dread when I looked at it.

I tried to cool myself off in the shower, but I couldn't stop thinking about the way it had made me feel. My mother had always told me I should trust my gut, and my gut was telling me, right about now, there was something seriously strange about the car that seemed to want to make me scared to step out of my own front door.

But, as I waited for my date to start, I tried not to think about it. If I was really freaked out by it, then I could always ask Karl to come and stay over at my place that evening. That was the sort of thing boyfriends did, wasn't it? It was still strange to think of him as my boyfriend, but I supposed there was no other way to put into words what was happening between us. We were dating. We might not have put a label on it yet, but I knew it wouldn't take long until we got there, and I was already looking forward to the part that came next.

Soon enough, the time had ticked away, and I was ready to head out of there and get down to the date I had been looking forward to all week long. My skin was itching for his touch, and I knew, from the messages he had been sending me all day, he felt just the same way. Changing into a pair of higher heels and a tighter dress, I flipped my hair at myself in the mirror and got myself ready to go out. Yeah, I was looking good. I was going to rock this night. The same way I rocked every single night with him. We were going to have an amazing time, and I wasn't going to let that car stick around at the back of my head for another instant. I had no reason to be worried, and I wasn't going to let myself stress about something I had no control over one way or another. So, some people were driving on the street where I happened to live. So what? I was a big girl, I could handle it.

My phone buzzed to let me know my cab had arrived and was waiting for me just around the corner. I headed down the street, and instantly felt the hairs on the back of my neck stand up. I ignored the churning in my guts and continued to walk. Keep going. One foot in front of the other...

And then I felt it. The rough cloth being shoved over my head, the way it strained back against my skin. I tried to catch my breath – but it was too late. Whoever it was, they had me. And there was nothing at all I could do to fight it.

15

KARL

I SAT THERE AT THE RESTAURANT, LOOKING AROUND, WONDERING where the hell she was.

Abi and I were meant to be meeting for a date that evening, but she had left me sitting at the restaurant, waiting for her to turn up, and I knew something was off. She wouldn't ever leave me waiting, and the fact she had – well, okay, it had started to get me worried.

A testament, I supposed, to just how much I had fallen for her these last few months. I couldn't get enough of her, to the point where the very notion of her dumping me was already starting to get under my skin. I hated that. I hated that she was already so far into my head that I felt like I was losing control just being apart from her. And I hated most of all that I totally loved the feeling of needing her, of needing someone in my life, after so long trying to deny I had ever felt that way before as long as I had lived.

The two of us...we just made sense together. That was the only way I could think to put it. When I was with her, everything seemed to slow down, like the world was letting me catch my breath. I spent most of my life at top speed, but when it was just the two of us, there was something about it that just seemed...slow. And not in a bad way. Like I could finally take a second and just enjoy the company of a woman who I couldn't get enough of.

Before her, my consumption of women had always been full-speed-ahead, always looking for the next person who would give me what I needed, always pushing for the next thing, the next kink, the next act. But now that I had found her, now that we had accepted this thing might actually work, it was like I could just stop for a hot second and work out what I actually *liked*. Not just chasing down what I hadn't tried yet, as a matter of course. I had done so much just to say I had done it, but with her, I could stop and think about what I wanted to do again. And again, and again.

But right now, she was keeping me waiting, and I couldn't for the life of me work out what I had done to get threatened with being stood up in this way. This wasn't the way she functioned, never had been, and I would have been lying if I'd said I wasn't starting to worry, just a little. I wanted to think. I wanted to see her and ask her what was going on, but my brain was too over-full with worry to stop myself. She still hadn't said those three little words back to me, and that had nagged at the back of my brain, a reminder that, just maybe, she didn't feel the same way about me as I did about her.

Because Abi was never late. Not in all the time I had known her, and certainly not for a date I knew she had been looking forward to all day long. Something was really strange, and I had no idea what it was.

Maybe she was just making me wait a little longer in the hopes of getting me hot and bothered. But she knew she didn't have to do that to get me where I needed to go. She could have just waved in my direction, and I would have been down to do anything she wanted me to do. This was out of character. And I was sure there was something amiss with all of this.

I got to my feet, headed over to the host so I could talk to him – maybe she had called ahead and told him she would be running late, and he had just forgotten to tell me or something.

But when I asked, I was met with a slightly baffled shake of the head.

"Sorry, sir, we haven't heard anything from her," he replied, and I pressed my lips together with annoyance. It wasn't his fault, but I felt the urge to snap at him nonetheless. Where the hell was she? And what was she doing keeping me sitting around for her company like this?

I took my seat, even though it felt as though the soles of my feet were burning. I couldn't just sit here. I needed to go out and do something, find out where the hell she was, because I had no clue what she was trying to pull right now. And I was starting to get worried.

I headed outside, pulling my phone out of my pocket and calling her quickly – her voice came down the line, and, for a moment, I felt a rush of relief, until I realized it was just her answering machine message. Shit.

I dropped my phone back into my pocket, pacing back and forth as I tried to burn off the excess panicked energy that was starting to take control of me. She wouldn't have done this to me. Not a chance in hell. And if she had, maybe that meant she was done with me once and for all, and I didn't know if I could cope with the thought of having lost her – not when I felt like I was just finally starting to get what I wanted from the two of us.

A moment later, and much to my relief, I heard my phone buzzing in my pocket, and I pulled it out and checked to see who it was – sure enough, it was Abi calling me back. I let out a sigh and told myself off for letting myself get so stressed-out about all of this. I needed to take a damn break from worrying about her.

She was a grown-ass woman, and she knew how to handle herself, and she would always make sure she didn't leave me sitting around and waiting for her to turn up.

"Hey," I greeted her, a smile on my face, as I prepared to hear her voice down the line again. I felt a little prickle on the soles of my feet in anticipation, and I couldn't help but grin at how infatuated I was. Okay, dude, you have it. You have it bad.

"Karl," a voice spoke my name down the line, a voice I couldn't place for a moment – a voice I knew didn't belong to Abigail. I had heard her in everything from a whisper to a moan to a cry, and I would have recognized her anywhere along that path. But it wasn't her voice.

"Karl, is that you?" the voice demanded again, and I closed my eyes and pinched my nose between my fingers. I knew who that was. I was sure of it. I just needed to place them, keep them talking...

"Yes, it's me," I replied bluntly. "What's going on? Where's Abigail? Why do you have her phone?"

"You really thought it would just be over like that?" the voice replied, a mocking edge to it now, as though the person was enjoying my distress and confusion. It was a woman. But it wasn't someone I worked with – I would have recognized Julia's voice on the other end of the line, but no, it wasn't her...

"Tell me who this is," I demanded. "Right now. Where's Abigail? I want to talk to her..."

"Oh, you can talk to her," the voice replied, and I heard a rustling down the line and then a voice that, finally, I knew.

"Karl?" Abi called to me. Her voice echoed around her, like she was in some chamber.

"Abi, it's me," I replied. "What's going on? Where are you? Are you alright?"

"I don't know where I am," she replied, and I could hear a

catch at the back of her throat. Had she been crying? I knew it must have been serious.

"Who are you with?"

"Kim," she replied, and that's when it hit me – where I knew the voice from, where I had heard it before. Of course I knew who it was. Because she had worked for me, too. Not for a long time now, but she had worked for me. And now, she had her hands on Abigail, and I was pretty fucking sure it was anything but good news.

"Yeah, she's with me, Karl," Kim replied, and I could hear Abi calling my name from the other end of the line, her voice wracked with pain. I hated myself for not being able to do more. I wanted to shout her name down the line, tell her I was coming, but I didn't know what I was meant to do or say next.

"And you're going to need to come right down here and get your girl back if you want her," Kim continued. "I'm going to send you an address, and you're going to come down here with every bit of cash and every credit card you have. Do you understand me?"

"What are you doing to her?" I demanded, but my voice cracked and I couldn't keep the threat in my tone for a moment longer. No. No, no, no.

"You thought you could just make me go away?" she demanded. "Yeah, sorry, it doesn't work like that. You come down here in the next two hours, or there's going to be a whole lot of mess for you to clean up when you get here. Tell the cops and we'll do what we have to, okay?"

"Okay," I said, my head spinning, heart pounding. This couldn't be real. None of this could be real. I just wouldn't accept it as real, not for a second, not for an instant...

And with that, the phone went dead in my hands. I nearly dropped it to the sidewalk below me in shock, but then I remembered the address I had to go to was coming through in a moment, and I caught it before it slipped out of my grip. Sure enough, it didn't take long until the address had popped up on my screen, and I strode down to my car to head down there as soon as I could.

Abigail. I couldn't stop thinking about that catch in her voice, the pain she was trying to hide from me. I didn't know what the hell Kim had done to get her out there, if she had hurt her, what she was going to do to her, but I had to keep her safe. There was no way I was going to let her suffer on my account. There was no way I was going to let her suffer at all, period. I loved her. And that meant I was going to protect her.

I tore out of there, down the street, trying to figure out how long it would take me to get there. My head was too panicked to think about anything logical, like getting help. I had to be with Abi. I had to keep her safe. I had to get that fucking bitch Kim away from her. I didn't care what it would take, I was going to make it happen. And nothing on earth was going to stop me taking care of what needed to be done right about now.

16

ABIGAIL

I came to, taking a moment to try to work out where the hell I was. I felt groggy, as though I was waking up from a night of drinking or something. Where the fuck was I...?

"Oh, she's awake," a woman's voice remarked. It took me a moment to recognize it, and it wasn't until the bag that had been roughly tossed over my head was ripped off that I found myself realizing just who the hell had taken me here.

"Kim?" I said, furrowing my brow and staring at the woman in front of me. It was her, really her. I had never seen her this close up, and it almost felt surreal to see her in front of me – I went to reach out and touch her, to see if she was really there, but then I realized that my hands were bound behind my back. And that was when the panic set in.

"Where am I?" I demanded, trying to twist my hands free from the bindings that were holding them in place. They were already cutting into my skin, what felt like plastic threatening to shred my wrists. The chair I was tied to was flimsy, plastic, but strong enough to keep me where they wanted me to stay.

"Stop moving," a man's voice commanded me, sounding annoyed, and my stomach dropped.

"Who is that?" I demanded, trying to turn so I could see who had just spoken, but I couldn't make out who was standing there behind me. My heart was pounding in my chest. I knew this was bad. Seriously bad. But I couldn't work out just why I was finding myself at the center of this badness when I hadn't done a damn thing wrong.

"Just stop," Kim snapped at me. She seemed annoyed at the fuss that I was making. I didn't care. I wanted to climb out of this seat and punch her in her puffed-up, lip-filler-full face. What the hell was she doing to me? Why the hell was I here? I needed to get out. I needed to get out before they did something that I couldn't...

"How long until he gets here?" Kim asked the man behind me, and I craned my neck to get a look at him – he was short and huge, looking about six feet wide, his head shaven and a tattoo snaking up from under his shirt on to his neck.

"He has until the end of the hour, babe," he told her, and it was clear he had already repeated this to her a hundred times already. As though he wished she would just accept it by now. Babe? Did that mean this guy was involved with her?

"He's taking too long," she whined, and I honestly thought she was going to stamp her foot on the ground and throw a tantrum like a little girl. She was pathetic, she really was – I didn't know how the hell this guy could put up with her. She seemed like a living nightmare.

And a nightmare I happened to be in the middle of right now. Who were they talking about? Who was coming? I would have bet it was Karl – he was the one with the money she seemed to want to get her hands on, and I doubted she would be in any rush to back up and let someone else get their hands on it. Was that why they had taken me? Because they were ransoming me back to Karl to try to make back the cash she had lost out on when he had shot down that bullshit case she had tried to bring against him?

I looked around as the two of them talked – I seemed to be in an apartment, a slightly dank space without any furniture and with only one small window that looked out on to the gray sky beyond me. The oppressive weight of being stuck here was already beginning to weigh down on my head. I hated this. I just wanted to get out. But I had no idea how in the hell I was meant to do that, when I was bound to the spot and they were hardly about to just up and let me walk out without paying the price on my head.

I tried to listen in to what they were saying, but they were talking in harsh, hushed tones, and I could only catch a few words here and there, not enough to piece together a story. I almost wanted to tell the guy that getting involved with Kim was only going to end with him meeting an untimely death sooner rather than later, but hell, he probably already knew that as it was. No way he couldn't understand her history. Maybe he thought she would be different with him – or maybe he planned to take the cash and run the first chance he got. That would have been a twist. In my panicked, hysterical state, I had to stifle a laugh at the thought of it.

How long had they kept me here? I had no idea how they had managed to get me to this place without my taking in anything of the trip that had brought us here. Had they drugged me? Probably. That would explain why I was still so groggy. And that might explain why I felt a sudden rush of calm in that moment, as I tried to weigh the options of what I could do next.

I needed to get out of here. I peered around, trying to see the door, but it was locked and latched and clearly bound shut so nobody could get in or out without the say-so of the gruesome twosome right there. Shit. Shit, shit, shit. I didn't want Karl to come to this place. I got the feeling they wouldn't be too keen on letting either of us out just like that, and my body was starting to tense up with the panic, with the thought of what had to come next. My skin was crawling, and the bonds on my hands seemed to be getting tighter and tighter as I tried to work out what I needed to do to escape.

And that's when I saw it. The gun. Glinting, black metal, on a small counter that jutted out from the wall opposite me. I had no idea who it belonged to or how it had gotten there, but shit had just gotten serious. Neither of them seemed to be paying attention to it, as though they had no reason to give a shit that it was right there in front of them. I had no idea how they could be so casual. I had never seen a gun up close and personal outside of the hands of someone who was meant to have one, and there was something deeply unsettling about the sight of it, just sitting there, as though it belonged in that spot.

"I hear a car," Kim exclaimed, and she barged past me to the small window so she could peer outside.

"It's him!" she added, her face lighting up – well, as much as it could, given the profligate amount of Botox she'd clearly had done over the years. Her whole head seemed as though it was frozen solid. It almost would have been funny, if it weren't for the terror that was demanding the attention in my body right now.

"Get the gun, stand by the door," she ordered the man who was with her. He did as he was told. Another man she seemed to have entirely and utterly under her thumb. How did it feel to him, I wondered, to know this woman would have tossed him aside in a moment if it meant she could get more money working with someone else? Maybe he tried not to think about it. It was the only way I could see him getting through the mess he had made of his life. I didn't even want to think of everything that had brought him to this moment, how many mistakes he must have made along the track to land himself in such a mess.

"He's coming out...he's coming up..." Kim tracked Karl's movements out loud, and I felt a grip of panic in my guts as I realized he was really about to walk into this room. He was going to be faced with that gun – did he know what he was about to put himself in the middle of? I wished I could call out to him, tell him to turn around and walk away once more, but it wasn't like I could stop what had started. I needed to find some way to slow him down, to slow this down. My mind was racing. I watched as Kim undid the latches on the door, my heart pounding so hard in my chest I was surprised neither of the two of them seemed able to hear it.

I heard his footsteps and my whole body tensed. No. No. I couldn't let him walk in there and get himself hurt. I needed to do something to save him. Anything...

As soon as I heard the footsteps slow outside the door, I did the only thing I could think of to do. I kicked my chair back, letting it land with a thump on the floor.

"Karl!" I shrieked at the top of my lungs, as I heard the door opening. I could hear a flurry of footsteps, could see stars where my head had hit the floor.

"Karl, he has a gun!" I cried out, but before I could say anything else, Kim was yanking me back upright, roughly, pulling the chair back upwards so she could look me in the eye.

"Don't think for a fucking second you can stop this, bitch," she snarled to me. I tried to turn and get a look at what was happening by the door, but she had angled me away from it. I could hear some sort of scuffle, a couple of men grunting, but it was more than just after-club throw-downs; there was a gun involved. And I got the feeling the fucker who was brandishing it wouldn't waste another second in pulling the trigger if he got the chance.

"Stay back, Kim!" the man called to her, and there seemed to be genuine concern in his voice. I wished I could have told him he didn't have to spend a second thinking about her. That she would have been the first to toss him under the bus if she got the chance. My skin was crawling, my head still pounding, and I could hear the mechanical clink of the gun – a bang, a thud, a grunt. Who was making those noises? Who was...

And then it came. A gunshot. Crashing out through the room around us. So loud it left a ringing in my ears. I couldn't even hear myself speak as I screamed Karl's name. I watched as the gun clattered along the floor in front of me, still totally helpless, wishing I could see what had happened, that I could just turn and get a look at the mess that was behind me.

But before I could, I watched in horror as Kim snatched up the gun before me. She fumbled with it for a moment, and I was sure I could see tears streaking her cheeks, but my vision was so blurred I could hardly see straight. Her jaw was clenched, I knew she was serious. I tried to push the chair away from her, but it was hopeless. If she wanted to do anything to me, then she had me right where she wanted me. I felt my breath catch in my throat. There was nothing I could do. Nothing I could do...

"You fucking bitch," she snarled at me. I could hear that, the venom in her voice impossible to ignore. But I could hardly pay attention to it. Karl – was Karl alright? Was he hurt? Was he alive? I needed to know, but I couldn't tell a damn thing all strapped down to this chair. I tried to squirm away, but it was too late. There was nothing I could do to stop this. I squeezed my eyes shut, hoping if I didn't have to look down the dark eye of that gun, I might be able to pretend that none of this was actually happening.

The click of the gun. Everything seemed to slow down. I could hear the blood rushing in my ears. I could make out the stark, sharp pain in my guts. This was it. This was how it ended. And, with those thoughts coursing through my head, I listened to the last few seconds of life that I would ever get to experience.

Then they were punctuated with the crack of a gunshot. And everything went black.

17

KARL

"Fuck!" I exclaimed, as the bullet caught me in the shoulder – the pain was there, but secondary, the only thing I cared about the fact that I had managed to put myself between Abigail and the fucking gun.

As soon as the shot went off, it was as though Kim's resolve went with it – the gun slipped out of her hand, and she began to shake, as though this was the last thing she had actually expected to happen. Well, I wasn't going to waste any more time waiting for an excuse to strike. Diving towards her, I knocked her over, pushing her hard enough that she bashed her head loudly on the window frame behind her. It took a second for her to pass out totally, but soon enough, she was slumped down against the wall, a trail of blood leaking down from the back of her head.

Good. That was all I cared about. My shoulder was throbbing with agony, but I could hardly pay attention to it. I turned to check on Abi, and my heart dropped when I saw she was passed out on the chair.

"Abi!" I called to her, grasping her by the shoulders. This was it – the worst part of this day. The helplessness I felt when I saw her limp form in front of me, it was enough to send pain coursing to every nerve ending in my body. I wrapped my arms around her, held her tight, squeezed her close to me.

"Abi, please wake up," I said to her. I didn't know what they had done to her before I had gotten there, but I knew I would turn the world upside-down to find out. Both of them were over and done with, but if they had hurt Abi, too, I would chase them down to hell just to make sure they kept on suffering.

I held her in my arms, leaning my head into her shoulder, silently praying she was going to come back to me. I didn't know what else I could do. I just...I just needed her. My body ached for hers, my mind cried out to hear her voice once more. Anything and everything I could do, it wasn't going to be enough. I needed to hear her voice again. I would have done anything...

"You're bleeding on me."

"Abi?"

"You're bleeding on me," she said again. Her voice sounded a little groggy, but it was her – I pulled back so I could look her in the eye, and, sure enough, she was gazing at me with this slightly amused expression on her face. I realized she was talking about the bullet wound that was dripping blood down her arm, and I pulled back at once to try to keep it from messing up her clothes.

"Sorry," I said, and she shook her head.

"You just saved my life," she said, and she reached out to touch me on the cheek. "I don't think you ever have to apologize for anything ever again."

"I'm going to hold you to that," I told her, and I wrapped her up in my arms and squeezed her tight. She was alive. She was alive, and that was all that mattered.

"What happened to the guy?" she asked, and I shook my head.

"Dead, I think," I replied. "He...I didn't mean to shoot him, but when I got hold of the gun, that was just all I could think of to do."

"Good," she spat. "It's what the two of them deserve..."

I realized her hands were still bound behind her back, and I hurried to get them undone. She reached to touch my cheek as soon as they were free and gazed into my eyes for a moment.

"Are you alright?" I asked her, cupping her face in my hands and scanning her eyes for any sort of indication she had been hurt. I knew I needed to take care of the wound in my own shoulder, but it was hard to give a damn about that when I just wanted to know she was safe.

"I'm okay," she replied. "I just...I love you, Karl."

It was the first time she had said those words to me, and it was the very last situation I had expected to hear them in. I had just taken a bullet for her, thrown myself in front of a gun that was meant to take her life. And I knew I would never find a clearer way to tell her I felt just the same way she did. I loved her, and I would have risked my life to make sure she stayed in mine.

"I love you, too," I replied, and I kissed her, softly, on the mouth – she winced, and I pulled back at once.

"We need to get you to a hospital," I fussed over her.

"I think we need to get *you* to one first," she replied, nodding at the wound on my arm. "You need to get that taken care of."

"Let's call the cops, the ambulance, all of them," I suggested. "And then we can get the hell out of here."

"Agreed," she replied, and I offered her a hand so she could stand up. She was still a little wobbly on her feet, but she was happy to lean on me. And I would have done anything to help her in that moment.

We sat on the step outside the house as we waited for the cops to arrive; it didn't take long before all the emergency services were there to take statements and blood work and check for concussions and deal with my bullet wound.

"You're going to look like a total badass with that thing, you know," Abi remarked to me in the hospital, as soon as I was out of being stitched up and having the bullet removed.

"You say that like I wasn't before," I replied, and she smiled at me. She had a mild concussion, they said, but nothing that a couple of days of rest and careful countenance wouldn't fix. And I was planning to give her at least the next month off work to recover.

"I'm so sorry you had to go through that for me," she blurted out. She was sitting on one of the plastic orange chairs in the waiting room, in a paper robe and a pair of sweatpants she had managed to get her hands on, and she looked so sad and so small and so lost in the moment that I wished I could have reached into her brain and taken the weight of what she was feeling away from her.

"You have nothing to be sorry for," I said back. "You didn't do anything wrong. And either way, it's over now. Kim's been arrested, and by the time she wakes up, she's going to have a lot of questions to answer about what happened to her other husbands. Really, you've given them justice, too. You should be proud of yourself."

"I wish I could feel that way," she replied. She managed a small smile, but I could tell it was a strain for her.

"I think you need to come back to my place and get something to eat," I told her. "How about takeout? You can pick the place."

"Only if we get enough to demolish the entire takeout industry in one go," she replied, yawning. "We were meant to go for dinner tonight, remember? I'm starving."

"Then let's order from five different places at once just to make sure you get everything you want," I suggested, and she laughed.

"Now, that sounds like a plan to me."

I reached over and took her hand, guiding it to my lips, and planted a kiss on the back of it.

"I love you, Abi," I said to her, and she smiled back at me.

"I love you, too, Karl."

And I knew that, as long as those words were true, everything else would be just as it needed to be.

EPILOGUE
ABIGAIL

"Do you have everything we need for the meeting?" I called to him, as I leafed through all the files that we were meant to be taking down to the conference in just a few hours.

"We have everything we need," Karl assured me, as he emerged from the bathroom, drying off his hair and totally naked and totally, utterly distracting.

"Hey, you're going to need to put some clothes on before we get out of here," I joked to him, and he cocked an eyebrow at me.

"Oh, do I?" he replied. "Because judging by the way you were looking at me, I'd say you like what you see right now."

"We're meant to be working," I giggled, but when he tossed the towel aside and wound his arms around me, pulling me close, I knew that any professionalism I might have been clinging onto was about to vanish.

This always happened when the two of us were traveling together. This particular conference, we had been working to present the company's latest product release – a personal alarm that allowed women to keep in contact with the people who were looking out for their safety. It was still just a prototype, but it had already gotten coverage in a few major industry magazines and I knew it wouldn't take long until people were jumping at the chance to prove they wanted to support us in this new endeavor.

I was proud we were putting something out there I knew was going to help so many women – it was just what I would have wanted if I had known what I was going to have to deal with when I had been snatched by Kim and her bullshit boyfriend. I had been lucky enough to have someone like Karl come after me to keep me safe, but not everyone would have the same luck, and I wasn't going to let anyone else deal with such a horrendous situation.

Now that Kim was behind bars, I spent a lot of my days feeling a whole hell of a lot better about everything that had happened the year before. Sometimes, I still found myself waking in the night, the sound of that gunshot filling my mind, but then I would turn over and see Karl lying next to me and I would know I was safe. That I had nothing to fear. I had even given evidence against her in person in court, making sure I gave them everything they needed to put her away for life – her boyfriend had died on the scene, but she probably didn't even care about that. I had no doubt she had been planning to get rid of him the first chance she had gotten, anyway. The poor fucker.

She had gone down for kidnapping and extortion charges, but pretty much everyone out in the real world seemed to accept she had been involved with the deaths of her husbands, too. She was guilty now, guilty to everyone who was paying attention, and guilty of everything she had tried so hard to hide for such a long time. The day I watched her get taken out of the court after the judge had read the declaration, it was everything I had needed to put to bed all the emotions that had demanded my attention all this time. I could be at peace. At last. Finally.

Karl had insisted on my taking some time off work to recover – even though I had tried to tell him I didn't need to, he had made it pretty clear the office was closed to me until I was firmly back on my feet. He even invited me to come stay with him while I was getting over everything that had happened, and, within a few weeks, it had become clear he didn't want me to leave. He fussed over every detail, making sure I was as well as I could be, taking into account anything and everything that might have caused me discomfort or doubt or grief.

That was just what good Doms did, he explained to me; when it came to being dominant, it wasn't just about sex. It was about care. It was about showing the other person you would go to any lengths to make sure they were safe and comfortable and happy, and they were living the life they wanted to live more than anything in the world. It was such a gift, his control over me, especially at a time like the one that followed my kidnapping. I would never have given myself the space and time to truly heal from what had happened, but with him by my side, it wasn't like I had a whole lot of choice. He made sure I knew I was cared for, and it was such a relief not to have to fear anything from him, or from myself. I could get better. I could let myself recover. And that was exactly what I did, before I finally came back to work a few weeks later.

People at the office knew about us now, and frankly, I didn't really care one way or the other. In fact, I enjoyed being the center of such fun gossip for a change. People snuck in a few questions here and there about what was going on between us, but, for the most part, they seemed to accept that chasing after the juicy details from their boss wasn't the way to go about getting on his good side.

I had started working as more than just his lawyer – now, the two of us were pretty much co-conspirators on running this place in general. I pitched ideas, I helped with product launches, I was there on his arm at glitzy parties to answer any questions potential investors might have had. And I loved every moment of it, because I knew he wanted me right there by his side for everything. He wanted me to be there, because he couldn't imagine sharing it with anyone else. Sometimes, when he looked at me, I felt so lucky it was as though I could just burst on the spot. What had I done to deserve a man so devoted to me? And how could I make sure nothing ever got in the way of that?

In the hotel room, he kissed me, running his hands up and under the smart skirt I had been wearing in preparation for the meeting we were meant to be heading to. I knew he always liked to see me all dressed up like this, and nothing served to drive him crazier than the sight of me all ready to go and be professional somewhere that had nothing to do with him.

"Mmm," he groaned, as he sank his hands into my ass. "You really think I was just going to let you walk out of here without having a little fun first?"

"And what kind of fun did you have in mind?" I asked. He grinned at me, that dangerous smile that told me he had so much on his mind he didn't know where to start.

"I'm more of a show, not tell, guy," he replied, and he guided me back on to the bed, reaching up under my skirt to pull my panties down. With his fingers, he pried open my mouth, and I parted my lips obediently so he could push my underwear between my lips.

"Something to keep you quiet," he said. "Wouldn't want the rest of this building knowing how horny you are, would we?"

I couldn't make a noise back to him, but he didn't care. And honestly, at that point, neither did I. When he was taking control, nothing mattered to me but the urge and the drive to do everything I could to please him. I would have probably jumped on to the balcony stark naked if he had wanted me to, if he had told me it would make him happy or turn him on.

He pushed my skirt up, flipped me over, and grasped my hips so he could pull me against his hard cock. He rubbed himself against me slowly, up and down, taking his time, and I moaned helplessly against the panties that were filling my mouth. I couldn't make a sound. Not that I would have said anything to stop him, anyway. Whenever I was feeling stressed about a meeting or a conference, it was like the only thing that could take the weight off was the feeling of him taking control of me.

"You're already so wet," he said, as he pushed his hand between my legs and roughly penetrated me with two fingers. "You want this, don't you?"

I made another moan against the panties, and he stroked my hair, a little patronizingly.

"Oh, yeah, sorry, I forgot I gagged you already," he remarked. I wiggled my butt back and forth against him, telling him every way I still could that I wanted to feel him inside of me.

And, finally, at last, I felt the pressure of his cock-head against my slit. The rush of it, the relief, that was all I needed for a split second – my whole body felt like it was on edge, trembling at the precipice of the release I knew I needed so badly. He took his time, filling me slowly, as though he knew how desperate I was and wanted to see just how much more needy he could make me.

"Mmm," he groaned, as he ran his hands over my ass and took hold of my hips. "You look so good like that, Abi."

When he said my name, it was like he had given me twenty commands in a row, told me just how he wanted me and just what he needed. I began to push back against him, desperate for the feel of his dick filling me all the way up. But before I could take what I needed, he inched out again.

"This is on my terms, remember?" he told me, as he gripped a little tighter onto my hips to keep me in place. "And fun as it is to watch you fuck me, I don't think that's how this works..."

And, with that, he began to drive himself into me. It was

merciless, the way he took me, rough and hard, filling me up over and over again. He felt so good that I could sense my brain beginning to close off those routes to stress and tension and panic; all that mattered was that he wanted me, and I could give him everything he needed in the process. I gripped tight onto the covers below me, holding on for dear life, trying to keep myself still so I could feel the full length of him pushing into me over and over again.

"Fuck, you take my cock so well," he said, and he slowed a little, his thrusts taking a more languid pace as he leaned over me so he could see the look in my eyes. I turned my head so I could gaze up at him, and I knew that was all he needed to get where he had to go.

"Mmm," he groaned again, and this time, he started going harder and faster, his flesh coming into mine so hard I knew it would leave marks. But the pain didn't register with me. Not when the pleasure was all I cared about.

The rush of it felt like it took control of me. And that was what I needed, sometimes – someone who could take the edge off what I needed, what I wanted, and remind me I was still a human being who had needs and wants and desires and the ability to give and receive all the pleasure I could. I was pushing myself back against him, hungrily, over and over again, taking him as deep as I could with every thrust, knowing he was close and that as soon as he came, I would be able to reach my own release too.

"Fuck!" he cried out, as I felt his cock twitch inside of me, filling me with his seed. Moments later, I felt my pussy contract around him as I reached my own release, the pleasure explosive as it coursed through every inch of my body. I felt myself begin to tremble, and then crashed forward onto the bed as he pulled out of me, landing a playful slap on my ass before he flopped down to join me.

"Damn," he said, and he reached over to smooth my hair back from my face before he hooked the panties out of my mouth. "Now I'm going to have to take another shower."

"Only if you take it with me," I replied, and he grinned.

"Well, on one condition," he replied, and I cocked an eyebrow as I splayed myself out on the bed beside him.

"Which is?"

"I get to keep these panties," he told me.

"You're going to get me in trouble, you know that?" I protested, but he just grinned at me, rolling over the bed so he could kiss me.

"I know," he replied. "But I'm worth getting in trouble for, aren't I?"

"I guess so," I muttered, and I smiled as I planted a kiss on his lips. He might have been a jerk, but he was the best kind of jerk, the kind of jerk who knew just what I needed to hear and when I needed to hear it.

I brushed my nose against his for a moment and smiled as I gazed at him.

"I love you."

"I love you, too," he replied, and he closed his eyes and planted a kiss on my forehead. "Come on, let's get you cleaned up."

"Hey, you say that like you weren't the one who made this mess in the first place..."

"Then I guess I'll have to clean up for you," he flirted back, and he offered me his hand. And, with a smile on my face, I took it. Because I knew that anywhere he would take me was where I wanted and needed to go.

MORE BOOKS BY JESSIE COOKE

Just like Grey Novels

Just like Grey Boxsets

Just like Grey Singles

Hot Mess - A One-of-a-Kind Romantic Comedy Action Adventure unlike anything you've ever read!

All My Books including MC Romance and Bad Boys at JessieCooke.com

Copyright © Jessie Cooke

All rights reserved.

No part of this book may be reproduced in any form or by any electronic or mechanical means, including information storage and retrieval systems, without written permission from the author, except for the use of brief quotations in a book review.

License.

This book is available exclusively on Amazon.com. If you found this book for free or from a site other than Amazon.com country specific website it means the author was not compensated and you have likely obtained the book through an unapproved distribution channel.

Acknowledgements

This book is a work of fiction. The names, characters, places and events are products of the writer's imagination or have been used fictitiously and are not to be construed as real. Any resemblance to people, living or dead, actual events, locales or organizations is entirely coincidental.

Printed in Great Britain
by Amazon